USA *Today* BESTSELLING AUTHOR

Dale Mayer

TERK'S GUARDIANS
SANDERS 07

SANDERS: TERK'S GUARDIANS, BOOK 7
Beverly Dale Mayer
Valley Publishing Ltd.

ISBN-13: 978-1-778863-14-1
Print Edition

Books in This Series:

Radar, Book 1

Legend, Book 2

Bojan, Book 3

Langdon, Book 4

Walker, Book 5

Reid, Book 6

Sanders, Book 7

Nate, Book 8

About This Book

Sanders hadn't been expecting a rescue from his own captivity. Now free, he can do no less than help Ania, another captive, someone he barely knows. Yet his connection to her had kept Sanders alive during his darkest times. He can do no less than help her now.

Ania must escape her father's total control. However, during Ania's first few days in confinement, her head had to clear of the drugs her father had been feeding her, just to keep her compliant and captive. After missing a dose, clarity now returning, Ania finally understands and bolts. But where can she go? She has no one. Until Sanders reaches out …

Meanwhile her father had put a psychic tracker on Ania's tail. Now Sanders and Ania try to hide, yet must find each other, … before her father locates them both.

PROLOGUE

S ANDERS OPENED HIS eyes, feeling the shudders rippling through his body. Once again one of the female healers was at his bedside. "Will I live?" he asked, a note of humor in his tone.

"You'll definitely live," she declared, "but I'm hearing rumors that some people may not be very happy that you escaped their custody."

He winced at that. "Will that cause you guys trouble?"

"That's not your problem," she stated firmly. "Your problem is making sure you're healthy."

"I'm doing much better," he noted. "I was thinking I could get up and come down for a meal."

"If you feel you're up to it, then do so." She eyed him carefully. "However, just a few minutes ago, you didn't seem to be up for it."

"I'm feeling much better now," he said.

She nodded. "I'll give you ten minutes to get dressed, and then I'll walk you down to ensure you're okay and can find your way."

"Is it that bad?"

"It's that bad," she confirmed, with a laugh to lighten the truth.

She closed the door behind her, and he quickly dressed in the clothing the woman had provided for him. He had no idea where he was, or when he got here. He knew this place was huge, and lots of people were here. They'd been looking after him since his rescue, but he didn't even know who all these people were. When he opened the door, she studied him carefully and nodded.

"You look like you're holding for the moment."

"Thanks," he said. "I was trying not to burn through too much energy."

"No, never a good idea," she agreed comfortably, as she walked downstairs at his side. When they entered this massive room with the largest table he'd ever seen in his life, all the conversations stopped.

Terk immediately stood and walked over to him. "Sanders, how're you doing?"

"Considering what I've been through, I think I'm doing just fine." He reached out a hand and shook Terk's. "I didn't get a chance to say it before, but thank you."

"You're welcome. Riff is the one who rescued you."

Sanders nodded at Riff, seated at the table. Then Sanders turned back to Terk. "Now, if only there was a way to go back and rescue somebody else."

At that, Terk frowned. "What do you mean, somebody else?"

"One of my jailers, his daughter has abilities, like us. She doesn't dare tell anybody, of course," he shared. "When she realized what I could do, we stayed in contact the whole time, without telling anybody, just to keep her safe, but she's desperate to get out of there."

"Where you were being held? Up north?"

"Yes, but her father moved her to the Baltic Sea area."

He nodded. "And you think that *you'll* go back and get her?" Terk asked.

Sanders winced. "If I can have another couple days to get my strength up, that would be ideal. I can't leave her behind, and I don't have much time to do that."

"How old is this daughter?" Clary asked.

He looked over at her. "Twenty-seven."

"So, she's not a child anymore."

"No, and she's lived in fear all her life. Her abilities are pretty strong. Apparently her mother did her best to keep them hidden, but her mother was killed a few months back, and her father's gotten more and more suspicious."

"Of course. Any strong gift like that will be revealed, and, although she's probably been good at keeping it contained, she's obviously slipped a time or two."

"Exactly, and I know her father. I also know that everybody there was looking for more psychics, and, if her father thought that he could curry favor by providing a bona fide one, his head position in the guard would be gold."

"What about his daughter? Does she want to leave her father?" Clary asked.

"Her father's the problem. Her mother is now gone, and, although he's been a good father, I think she's afraid he would give her up in a heartbeat to elevate his own position. Don't forget that, for these Russians, it's a point of honor. It's not a case of thinking that she would be hurt because, from his point of view, she would be in an exalted position as being special. She would be a *special* prisoner," he explained. "In her father's mind, as a female, she would always be somebody's prisoner, but he wouldn't call it *prisoner*. He would call it *their wife*."

"Ah, right." Clary winced. "God, I hate that mind-set."

"You might hate it, but it's prevalent in those patriarchal societies," Sanders said. "So I would very much appreciate a chance to build up my strength a bit and then get her out of there."

"Do you think you'll be up against much opposition?" Terk asked.

"It depends on whether her father has found out what she can do or not," Sanders replied, "but, in my heart, I would say, *absolutely.*"

"Why is that?" Terk asked. "Have you had any contact with her?"

He hesitated and then shook his head. "No, not since I was rescued. She cried out for me to run and to ensure that I got free and clear. When I asked her to come with me, she said that she was hurt, and she couldn't right then. No way she could get out at the time."

"So, presumably, she is still there then."

"I told her that I would come back for her," Sanders shared. "No way I can just leave her."

"I get that," Clary replied, as she looked over at Riff. "You up for heading back to that lovely region?"

"It's Estonia, so it's beautiful, cold in the winter, but it's a gorgeous part of the world. If she's there, we would have a much easier time getting her out because we would have the sea available." He looked over at Terk and shrugged. "I'm game."

"In that case, Sanders, get your strength back up, ensure you're grounded with somebody here, and we'll set up a plan to rescue her. And if she has abilities …"

"She does, very strong abilities," Sanders confirmed. "I'm just not sure they are things you can use."

"What do you mean?"

"She's a mind reader. She can look at you and repeat what you're thinking. But it's more than that. It's almost as if she can see different layers of you."

Terk stared at him, his head tilted to the side. "We certainly have various abilities here," he began, "but we've never seen that before. Still, it doesn't mean that's how it would stay either. The longer we all cohabitate in one place, the more we're becoming adept at hiding our personal feelings from the others, working through multiple conversations in our head at once, learning what privacy means among psychics, while gaining more gifts," he shared. "So, if she's got another ability for us to adapt to, I say bring it on." He looked around at the others.

"If she's in trouble, and she needs help," Clary stated, "I say, go get her."

"Exactly," her sister Cara agreed. "We came here because we were looking for a safe place to be *us*. So anybody else who needs a safe place to be themselves should be welcome too."

And, with that, everybody agreed.

Terk looked over at Sanders. "Looks like you're it. Give yourself three or four days, and you should be ready to go."

"With a little bit of help from the ladies here," he replied, "I would like to be ready to go in two." He looked at Cara and Clary.

They both nodded. "If she's in trouble, absolutely," they said in unison. "Plan to be out of here by then." They turned and looked at Riff. "Are you good with that?"

"Absolutely. Those bellies of yours are getting bigger, and I know Angela's on her way to deal with you and the other pregnant ladies. I sure don't want to be around when Angela shows up."

"We haven't forgotten our promise to you either," Terk pointed out. "We will find out who murdered your fiancée."

He stiffened at that. "I knew you hadn't forgotten. I just figured that we still don't have anything to go on."

"No, not yet," Terk agreed, "but not for lack of trying."

"I know. If it were that easy, I would have solved it already," he murmured, looking around at the people at the table. "I appreciate that you're all still trying."

With that said, Riff got up and walked out the door.

CHAPTER 1

SANDERS WILLMOTT SAT in the passenger seat and once again checked his GPS. "I can't say that our travels have been particularly simple," he murmured to Riff, who was driving this leg of their trip.

Riff shrugged. "Some of these ops are never easy," he noted. "We just ensure they're worthwhile. Ania helped you when you were in captivity, and we got you out of there. So now you will return the favor and will do what you can to help her."

Sanders shifted to look at him. "I never expected a rescue."

"Sometimes it happens, even when you least expect it. It's important to put that out there to the universe and to keep sending those messages. Somebody will find them, hopefully Ania."

"I know who gets my thanks in this case," he replied, with a smile.

"Multiple people," Riff clarified. "I didn't know you were in need. So, once we found out, we came," he explained, "and we'll do the same for Ania."

"I wish I could let her know we were coming," he murmured. "I can't reach her telepathically, which seems odd. She's in a black hole, and I just get a blank space from her."

"Maybe because she can't contact you, or can't receive

your messages?" Riff suggested.

"I would certainly think that's a legit possibility, but it's a distressing one. It could mean that somebody has found a way to contain her or to at least stop her from sending messages. Maybe even from receiving anything too. I blame her father. She was so afraid he would sell her to the highest bidder because of her gifts, which she kept hidden. Right before I was rescued, she had injured herself. She didn't tell me how. Yet thereafter she thought her father was drugging her, telling her it was antibiotics to stop some infection from her injury. Ania thought it was all a ruse to keep her at home."

"Keeping her drugged would definitely interfere with her gifts. Yet she could speak to you telepathically before?"

"Yes, she was quite good at it. Better than I was. I had to improve in order to speak to her, though maybe it was just a language barrier at that point in time. I don't know for sure."

"Lots of times language doesn't even come into it," Riff shared, shooting him a sideways glance, as he changed lanes. They were coming up to the main area of town ahead of them. "Now we won't be at the main city just yet," he stated. "I wanted to do some reconnaissance ahead of time, from just outside this small village."

Sanders looked around and nodded. "I don't know this area, so I'm not necessarily a big help right now."

"Yet you were in the navy, as I understand?"

"I was, but an injury sidelined me quite a few years ago. Once that happens, it's easy to lose your skills."

"Maybe for a time, but it's not so easy to lose all your instincts," Riff pointed out. "So just keep that skill honed and think about using the other skills that you have to try and reach her."

"I have been," Sanders muttered. "I've been sending out signals quite regularly, hoping she can hear me."

"She probably does hear you, but maybe she can't reply, which is another issue we'll have to deal with. If she's injured, she may not be mobile. So we must consider getting her out in another way, which may require some flexibility in our plans."

"If she's injured, it's all the more reason to get her out."

"I'm not arguing that," Riff declared. "Yet, if she's not ambulatory, it won't make our job any easier."

Sanders sucked in his breath at that thought. "You're right. I don't even know what I'm thinking,"

"The problem is you're *not* really thinking," Riff said, giving him a knowing smile. "By rights, you should be at home in bed. Do you think I don't know that you lied about how strong you were?"

He flushed. "Let's just say that this need, this strong drive to get Ania, has been constantly increasing," he admitted, "and I couldn't ignore it, even if I wanted to."

"Good for you that you're listening to it, but don't think for a moment that you fooled any of them."

Sanders frowned at him. "Sorry?"

"Don't think you fooled anybody on Terk's team, especially those healer women. They can see your energy levels in ways that you and I could never even contemplate. So I get that you think you're helping this rescue, but you're really not, especially if you don't come clean about everything you know."

"I don't even know anything," he replied, glancing at Riff. "Honest to God."

"And telling me the truth is a good thing. Otherwise I wouldn't be here."

"Right. So, we're back to the fact that everybody on Terk's team has abilities, and God help us if we end up lying. That can't be good to build trust."

"True. Since we all *do* have abilities, we often know if someone is lying or holding back, and that makes us very wary."

"Of course," Sanders acknowledged. "I just want to get Ania out of there."

"Do you have another reason?" Riff asked, with a small smile.

Sanders glanced at him. "What do you mean?"

"I want to ensure you have no revenge agenda or any other ulterior motive rolling around in your head."

"No. It's not about that. It's all about Ania." He felt Riff's gaze, like a laser searching his soul.

With a nod, Riff relaxed and replied, "Ah, that explains it then."

"Explains what?" Sanders asked, flushing.

"The drive inside you to save her. You really care about her."

He grimaced. "I don't even know Ania. However, because of that connection to her, I survived."

"Doesn't really matter, does it?" Riff noted, with a smirk. "Particularly in our world. Far too few of us are out there to do this energy work, and, when we do find people who are like us, a bond is created, an instant bond, that tends to transfer into an emotional bond—whether we like it or not. Therefore, we have feelings we didn't really expect to have. Trust me that it's happened before."

Sanders sat back and didn't say a whole lot. "Is that … Is that what happened to you?"

"Sure is," he snapped. "However, mine didn't have a

happy ending. Still doesn't, for that matter."

"Is that what you meant about Angela?"

He nodded. "I was engaged to be married. Angela would have been my sister-in-law, but then … my fiancée was murdered," he shared, his tone harsh. "Which is also why Terk mentioned trying to help me with that investigation. However, so far, we have no angle or lead to go on. Without that, we're just spinning our wheels. So, in the meantime, I'm doing something useful to help the rest of his team, while we try to churn up more information. Everyone is working to find a lead, so we can go after whoever murdered my fiancée."

"And Angela?"

"Angela is a very gifted doctor, an obstetrician—which is a good thing, considering the number of pregnant women in that castle." Riff gave a chuckle. "It's scary to see how many enlarged bellies are in that place, but, being who Angela is, she'll help them all."

"Yeah, I noticed the bellies," Sanders quipped. "I just didn't feel comfortable asking about it and wondered if maybe some baby factory was going on."

Riff burst out laughing. "I'm sure they would all be less than thrilled with your interpretation on that. Yet it's a valid observation, when you think about it. An awful lot is going on in the castle that you don't know about. Seems energy workers who are around other energy workers get a boost in their existing gifts, as well as pick up new ones. Now that Terk's team has been gathered together for a while, the pregnancies happened, almost all at once—another side effect to the energy workers all gathered together.

"It's a learning experience now, living at the castle, seeing what else is created there. Yet they've come a long way since they started setting up that place—rehabbing it, staffing it, getting supplies, even working on purchasing their own satellite. These guys and gals are good, the best, so, as long as they're all happy, I'm happy for them."

"Oh, I'm not unhappy by any means," Sanders murmured. "However, you're right. It was a little daunting to see all those pregnant bellies. Particularly as a single guy, as I've never really been around pregnant women."

Riff nodded, commiserating. "Exactly. Which is why I don't mind helping out, getting out of that castle and their baby-making group mentality. … Yet the fact that Angela is staying very close to me just adds to my pain, bringing up old memories."

"Right." Sanders wanted to ask more, but it was obvious that Riff was shutting down that sensitive conversation. It was understandable, and, if the guy's fiancée had been murdered, it had to be incredibly painful. As they drove up to a small bed-and-breakfast, Sanders nodded. "This looks like a good place to stay."

"Yeah, that was my thought."

"Do we have reservations?"

"No, we don't," he replied. "I wasn't really expecting to need any."

"Why is that?"

"I generally have good luck when I go to these places," he said, "so I can't see that this will be any different."

"Good luck, as in what?"

"As in getting reservations," he replied, with a knowing smile. "I find that when I need things, they're just there."

Sanders pondered that, as he walked into the bed-and-breakfast with Riff and they were given a room, facing the street, and they booked it for the night. As they walked up to their room on the second floor, Sanders asked Riff, "So, like that?"

"Exactly like that," Riff confirmed, with a complacent smile. "You never really know who or what will work out in life, but, if you expect it to work out, you'll find that it works out much faster."

"I'll have to remember that," he murmured. "So far, I can't say I've had too much luck along that line myself." He sat down in the nearest chair, clearly winded and sweating a bit.

"Every day is a new day, and right now you've been given a chance at a whole new life," Riff pointed out. "So the fact that you came back after Ania is admirable, just don't get your ass kicked in the process. I can't necessarily save you a second time, plus carry Ania out if needed too."

"Got it," Sanders noted. "Yet, as you mentioned, my instincts were still there, whether I realized it or not. I might have been off my game, back when I was recovering from my injury for quite a while," he added, "but I still remember my military training. And I'm still a newbie when it comes to my energy-working skills, but I'm fumbling through it for now."

"Good, because I may need to call on all you have to offer."

"I get that. Believe me that I understand this won't be an easy job. You already rescued me, and now we're heading right back into the middle of it."

"Considering we're a country away, hopefully we're not heading right back into the middle of the exact same scenario at least, but I also don't have any illusions that it'll be a walk in the park. Can you shed any light on why she's been brought here? That's something I don't understand."

"She has an aunt, and I know that she had been bugging

her father to let her visit, as a way to get out of the hot seat at home."

"But does she trust the aunt?"

"I did ask her that, and she just mentioned how she didn't have much choice, when it came to her relatives."

"That's not much of an answer, and not the sort that'll help us in any way," Riff murmured. "We've seen betrayal on family levels like you could never imagine," he noted, with a headshake. "So, I get that Ania thinks she's probably totally safe going there, but that doesn't work out for people like us. I, for one, wouldn't count on it."

"Which is distressing in itself, but I can't do anything for her, unless we can get to her."

"What gifts do you have?"

He hesitated. "Terk could tell you more than I can. And I definitely am looking forward to Terk teaching me all that I can learn about being an energy worker. Yet, right now, all I can do is telepathically communicate with Ania, obviously, and I did find I could amplify her energy."

Riff slowly turned, as he dropped his bag onto one of the two single beds. "What do you mean?"

"When Ania needed more energy, I could give it to her, but only if I knew where she was going. So I guess I send energy to places, not so much people, or something like that. I haven't really had a chance to put it to the test, except for sharing my energy with Ania. The Russians were testing me, for communications, sending messages more than anything."

"Your captors?"

"Yeah, I tried hard not to let them know about anything I could do, but I had to let them know something. So, it was more of a give and take. If I withheld too much, I risked not getting fed and literally not getting enough nutrients to even survive to see another day. I took several beatings because of it," he shared, his tone turning harsh. "So, it became a matter of trying to funnel as little information as I could, a little bit at a time."

"Right," Riff murmured. "It's always a problem when you've got these assholes who think they have a right to our brains, just because their own intellect is too tiny and insignificant to do what we do."

Sanders burst out laughing. "That's one way to look at it, but I'm not sure anybody out there would particularly like your take on it."

Riff grinned. "Probably not, but that doesn't make it any less true. I want to go for a walk around town. Are you up for it?"

"I'm up for it," Sanders declared, standing up but wobbling.

Riff frowned. "Might be better if you stayed here and rested. I need you to bring your A-game, and you need to rest."

He glared at him. "That may be true, but, if Ania's out there, yet weaker somehow, I might pick up any signals that she's sending while we walk around."

"I can pick up energy too," Riff noted calmly.

"I'm not exactly sure what you do," he admitted. "I mean, obviously you got me out of that hellhole. I just don't quite understand how."

"I'm a shadow," Riff stated, with a smirk. "Don't let it get to you. When it's time for you to figure it out, you'll get it. In the meantime, it's better if you don't know too much."

"You think I'll get recaptured?"

"I'm always thinking of that possibility," he agreed, with a nod. "Particularly if anybody here recognizes you from over there. If Ania happens to have any guards or jailers from Russia, or from her father's team of guards," Riff pointed out, "then you'll have to watch your ass. Because again, saving one person is possible, saving two is quite unlikely, especially if both of you are immobile. So, ensure you don't become a victim because I might have to leave you behind."

Sanders stared after Riff, but nodded, because he was right.

ANIA SLIPPED DOWN the hallway of her aunt's home, hearing raised voices at the front door, just inside the outdoor porch. However, with the front door closed, it was hard for Ania to hear the words. She was hoping if she made it up to her room, the discussion would be clearer. Nothing was good about her father's tone of voice, and the fact that he was here wasn't helping. She heard her aunt pleading with her father over something, but Ania didn't know what they were talking about and didn't like anything about it, especially when he slapped her aunt, who cried out in response.

Grabbing her sweater and her purse, Ania glanced at her still unpacked bag and realized it would be too big and too bulky to sneak out of here with. Her father's presence here was surely to force her home, and he wouldn't take no for an answer. So, if he wanted to talk to Ania, he would be all over her aunt. This was her mother's sister, which just added to the potential for control and conflict. Her father thought women were beneath him, were chattel, were property. It had become so obvious since her mother's passing.

Ania raced from her bedroom to the master bedroom,

where a small deck extended to the back of the property. She slipped onto the deck, taking the stairs to the backyard and racing to the tree line, hiding in the darkness—not that it was fully dark yet, but still, it gave her a little bit of a cover.

From here she stopped and thought about her options. She instantly felt guilt, leaving her aunt to her father's anger. Ania had heard the slaps her father had given to her mother, trying to hide them from Ania. The last thing Ania wanted was for her father to hassle her aunt for letting Ania visit. Her aunt wasn't strong herself, and her father was like a steam engine. He would run over everybody to get what he wanted. The fact was, if he wanted Ania, then nobody would stop him. No one would put themselves in his way. If someone did, they would die.

That thought made Ania gasp. Did her mother try to stop her father from selling Ania and her gifts to the Russian government? Did her mother die trying to protect Ania? Just the idea alone brought Ania to tears. She feared that was exactly how her mother had died.

The only way Ania had of stopping her father was getting away and finding some other avenue to leave the country. She had money in the bank, but she had to access it. She had credit cards, but she didn't dare use them, not while she was still in town. No point in looking for money in her aunt's house because her aunt didn't have much.

Slipping out the back through the neighbor's yard, Ania quickly picked up the pace and headed toward town and the bank, trying to stay undercover. She was careful, in case any of her father's cronies had come with him. Some of them probably had, since he rarely went anywhere alone anymore. It seemed like somebody was always attached to her father's hip.

He had a couple goons she could always count on being there beside him. If she could avoid those guys, chances were, she might make it out of this mess. The fact that he'd come, even though she had told him that she would be at her aunt's house, revealed a lot about his state of mind, and potentially how worried he was that she wouldn't follow through on her word. But, hey, that's the way her world was right now, and it sucked big time. Everything had blown up after her mother's death. Her father had become much darker, much more pro-government, more political, and had certainly looked at Ania sideways a lot in recent times, and that bothered her more than she cared to admit.

She couldn't explain so many things to him because he would not be open to it, and, even if he were, it was only because he could see how it would benefit him financially. Being female, Ania didn't have a whole lot of value in her father's eyes. If he'd had sons instead, now that would have been a different story. She knew that. Right or wrong, it was their culture. She'd heard the argument time and time again. Her mother had tried to protect Ania, and her father had been incensed when no sons had come along, no other children, in fact. Ania's father had more or less washed his hands of Ania and her mother, and just kept them along because they were his property.

Yet Ania had seen a lot of fairly similar marriages in her community, so she could hardly just blame her father. Regardless, she had no plans to ever join those ranks. Why would she? There had to be something in this for women, but that was missing from her mother's marriage. Once her mother had realized that Ania had talents, gifts, the one thing she had always warned Ania of was to never let her father know. But, once her mother had died, her father suddenly seemed to think he knew something of value. Whether her mother had kept a diary or had left a note for him to find after her death, Ania didn't know—or maybe her mother's note had been for Ania.

Her father wouldn't have shared the source anyway, and that just left Ania in the dark, trying to figure out what was happening in her life, how to deal with the loss of her mother.

Ania had journaled her feelings after her mother's death. At first it was just some word salad of all the emotions she felt. Then she had progressed into writing somewhat coherent streams of consciousness. When her father confiscated her journal, stating he had burned it, she knew her mother's notes or journals had surely suffered the same fate. No matter, Ania then took to social media, starting an online support group for those who were grieving the death of a loved one. She had been surprised to find its numbers growing.

In short order, it morphed into being more women-centric, focused on their gaining more power in the world, more rights, equitable treatment, all of which Ania could relate to as well. Plus the medical world had joined in, to discuss death and depression and related topics.

Ania's involvement in the social media element had grown out of her frustration to keep things from her father—he and his thugs were surely not reading posts on the internet—so she felt safe there. And thus a community for her and others was borne.

Thankfully another community for Ania, her schooling, had been completed before her mother's death could interrupt that. Ania had been going to university, working on getting a good education. She had completed her accounting degree, but her father had refused to let her move to the big city to get a job. That was another reason why Ania wanted to talk to her aunt, trying to get away and to get a job someplace where she could be free to utilize her skills. Her aunt, in the short evening that Ania had spent with her last night, had been enthusiastic—right up until Ania had mentioned that she didn't want her father to know anything about these plans. At that point her aunt had become fearful, and that should have been Ania's first warning.

Knowing that her aunt was afraid, Ania should have just gotten up last night and walked away and kept her aunt out of it. Because now? Now with her father here, it was too late—definitely for Ania, and possibly for her aunt. Ania kept moving, heading to the ATM at the bank. When she finally got near there, she noted a large black government rig driving down the street on the same side where she walked. She darted into a grocery store and stood at the window, watching. The vehicle went past, and she quickly exited and headed to the bank, slipping into the covered unlocked lobby with the ATMs. She was outside again within seconds. She had money now, though not enough to buy a plane ticket or a boat ride. Even if she did, where was she supposed to go?

She had her passport though, so that was a help. This was the money her mother had set aside secretly for Ania. So hopefully her father didn't know about this account at all. Once he did, he would be livid, trying to get the money back. Ania sighed, just another reason her father may have killed her mother.

Even though this wasn't a whole lot of cash, the secrecy behind this account gave Ania a chance at a new life and would have made her father so very angry. She'd been looking for work for many months in Russia, but every time she came up with something, her father kiboshed it. His last blowup had been when he flat-out told her to stop thinking about getting a job because he wouldn't let her go. At the time, he'd used the excuse that he only had one child, one family member left, and he didn't want her to move away. To Ania, it had come across as totally false, and she knew he was lying.

That bothered her even now because she had seen his sideways looks, checking to see if she'd fallen for his lies. She hadn't; she wasn't that foolish. Not now anyway, and hopefully not ever. She had come to acknowledge the worst about her father. If he caught her, she would do what she had to do in order to get the hell away again, though the truth remained that he would make damn sure it was difficult to leave, if not impossible.

She watched the big black car slowly pull out of a parking lot and head toward her again.

She realized that, no matter what she did, this wouldn't end well. She had to get the hell away, and she had to get away now, before her father realized what her plans were. It occurred to her that he'd only let her come here in the first place because he had his goons watching her. He probably figured that he would catch her unaware and then move her as he wanted, without anybody daring to stop him.

Ania shook her head. She had essentially been a prisoner for most of the last five years. While she had permission to attend the university, her father's goons were seen all around her. She had strict instructions to come straight home from her classes. Of course her father would not call her a prisoner. However, her mother had made it very clear how this would be Ania's life if she didn't get out, though her mother wasn't capable of helping Ania much. She would have to solve that problem herself or accept the reality of what her future would be.

When her mother had suddenly passed on, Ania had been so broken and so devastated to lose her mother that she hadn't even cared about her own plight. She just hadn't realized how serious her mother had been about these warnings.

But then in the ensuing months, it had been insidious but steady, as she watched her father very quickly remove whatever influence of her mother's that he could, slowly bringing Ania further and further into his world. When she balked, his backhand had been his instant reply. She'd been shocked and stunned that he would hit her, particularly since she was an adult woman. Then Ania finally realized how likely her father had continually abused her own mother. He was possibly now doing just that with her aunt.

Hating that she'd taken the chance and had come here and had put her aunt in trouble, Ania quickly headed toward a park, hopefully where the government vehicle couldn't find her. Slipping behind a couple big trees in the back, she pulled out her phone and called her aunt.

When her aunt answered, her voice was breathless, as she greeted her with a warning. "You need to run. … You *have* to run."

"Is he still there?" she asked.

"No, no. He's gone out looking for you. You were seen downtown, and now he's after you."

"Did he say what he wanted?"

"*He's taking you home, where you belong.*" Her aunt hesitated. "He made it sound like you weren't right in your mind, like you were a danger."

"What?" Ania cried out. "Why would he do that?" But,

in her heart, she knew that he would do it to control her even more. "He's wrong," Ania declared, beginning to feel hysterical. "You've got to understand that."

"I don't know what to believe," her aunt admitted. "You arrived out of the blue, looking for a way to get away from your father and to have a life. However, according to him, that's not what you wanted to do at all. He insisted that some medication backfired, and now you're a danger to yourself and others."

"I see," she stated, her tone turning formal. "He's wrong, but I can tell that there is no point in talking to you."

"Wait," her aunt called out, as Ania went to end the call. "I don't know what the truth is, but you're still my niece, and, if you need help, I'll try and help you. However, I don't have any control over him."

"No, nobody does," Ania agreed. "That's the problem. Nobody ever wins a fight with him. It's all right for him to beat us up and to treat us like we're nothing but commodities." Her aunt gasped. "Yeah, he hit you too tonight, didn't he?" she asked. "I'm afraid he totally abused my mother. I'm even more afraid that he killed her. So I'm very sorry. I never should have come here and dragged you in it." With that she hung up, without letting her aunt say anything more.

Ania had considered this earlier, but now she realized that all the medications the doctors had been prescribing for her for the last while, that she'd finally ditched on a whim, were probably drugs meant to help control her and to make her compliant for her father. She'd wondered and had played with the idea for a while. She realized that her mental clarity—which had improved so much over the last few days—appeared to be the result of her withdrawal from the drugs and wasn't merely a boost from the sense of purpose she felt, while planning her life. The truth was that she was off that medication, and she was thinking for herself again.

She understood why her controlling father would contemplate drugging her, but she sure as hell had no intention of ever falling back under his thumb again. Yes, she'd been devastated for a time. The loss of her mother had been such a shock to Ania, but she hadn't been suicidal, and she hadn't been a danger to herself or anybody else, and there'd been absolutely no need to drug her. That obviously wasn't her father's position, and now she had to ensure that he never got his hands on her. Yet who could help her?

Who was out there and was capable of helping, when her father was so powerful and had so much pull in the Russian government? That was the scary part. He could say jump, and there would always be people who would just jump solely because he had ordered it. While Ania couldn't imagine any of his goons finding joy in the work they did, her father took great pleasure in having that power, in wielding that power. He'd become a whole lot more drunk on that power over the last few months, so much more arrogant, so much more aggressive.

She didn't know whether he was taking any medications or *should* be taking some. Regardless, if he was on something, there had definitely been a huge shift in his attitude. She hoped he wasn't doing drugs because it would likely make him even more dangerous. Right now she'd already had about all she could handle from him. She again wished Sanders was around, even if just for the comfort she got when telepathically connected to him. She once again sent out a message to him, hoping that stopping her meds would allow her to send these messages.

Ania shook her head. Her father had told her that those

medications were antibiotics, after she'd hurt herself. Now she realized—as some messages were starting to filter through her brain, albeit weak and fuzzy—they weren't antibiotics at all but something much more. Something intended to help her father control her, which was very much more his style. It was sad that a father felt that he had to stoop so low in order to get his daughter to do what he wanted, but it was also very sad that he would want such a restricted life for her.

She didn't know what to do at the moment. She sat here in the park for the longest time, until she eventually realized that she would attract attention soon if she didn't get up and go do something. If she didn't find a way to get a move on, she may have no way out of this. With that thought, she quickly stood up and walked to the end of the park, still wondering what her options were. Just as she was about to step onto the sidewalk, she saw that same damn vehicle slowly driving toward her.

She stepped back into the shadows. Several other people watched the vehicle, some with fear, some with curiosity, some with just a wary eye, wondering who this person was in a fancy government vehicle and why they were still in town, wandering up and down their streets. She watched as once again the car went past. As soon as it was out of sight, she stepped out of the shadows and walked quickly to the bus depot.

CHAPTER 2

A NIA MADE IT to the bus depot without any problems. Yet, as she headed to the front counter to see when the next bus was leaving, she heard a conversation that made her blood run cold. A man, somebody she didn't recognize, at least from the back, stood talking to the ticket collector.

"No, we're looking for her because she's off her medications. There appears to be some kind of a reaction she's had, so we're doing what we can to find her." He had a picture in his hand, that he showed at the window.

Ania had no doubt from the look of him that he was somebody her father had hired. But the fact that they were showing pictures around town just made her position sketchier, if that were even possible. Yet what was she supposed to do? Swearing to herself, she hurriedly stepped back out of the way and waited until the person left the window.

She looked in the ticket booth and thankfully recognized a familiar face staring back at her. She raced up to the front counter and whispered, "Vanessa, was he looking for me?"

Her friend looked at her and then nodded. "What the hell's going on?" she whispered, looking around. "He says that you've had some medication that's gone wrong."

She shook her head. "No, my father's been drugging me to keep me compliant and immobile. He has got in his mind that's the way to control me."

Her friend's eyebrows shot up. "Oh, good God. You always wondered how far he would go."

"Too far clearly," she admitted, "but I have to get out of here. I have no choice now. Can you sell me a ticket?"

"I can, but nothing leaves until tomorrow morning."

"Shit," Ania muttered. "I need to stay out of sight, and he's already been to my aunt's, looking for me. She basically told me that I need to get away and to stay away."

"Yeah, you're not kidding." Vanessa looked at her sympathetically. "You can go to my place and stay there. Nobody's at home right now."

Ania eyed her hopefully. "You don't mind?"

"No, I don't. Your father's always been a bit ..." She stopped and didn't add anything after that.

Ania nodded. Her father had always been difficult and intimidating. Her friends never wanted to come over because he was a bigwig in the government, and not in a nice way. He was some enforcer, and everybody was scared of him. "What if he finds out what you've done?" Ania asked Vanessa. "You know it could be trouble."

"If you go there while I'm not home, then that's hardly on me, is it?" she asked. "Just get out of here, so I won't be seen talking to you. If you want a ticket, tell me right now, and I'll bring it home with me."

"What's leaving first thing in the morning?"

"One into the city, and you can get on that pretty fast. You could at least disappear into the city pretty easily."

"Good enough," Ania agreed.

And, with that, she slipped out the side door, using the backroads to quickly head to her friend's apartment. Ania hadn't asked for the keys, so that was a bit of an issue.

However, as she got to Vanessa's building, another mutual friend was just coming out of the locked gate.

"Hey, what are you up to?" her friend asked. "I haven't seen you in a while."

"I came to visit my aunt and to get away from my family for a while."

"Yeah, no kidding," she muttered. "You're here for Vanessa's place?"

"Yeah, and I forgot to get the keys from her. I was just down there talking to her."

"Not a problem, I'll let you in," she offered, with a chuckle.

"Are you still looking after this place?"

"It is my uncle's property, so, yeah, you could say that," she agreed, with a smile. And, with that, she quickly unlocked Vanessa's apartment and let Ania in.

If it had been anybody else, they probably would have been pissed, but Estonia was a small country, and most people understood. When somebody was in trouble, often they offered assistance immediately, without being asked, and that made life a whole lot easier for Ania.

As she stepped into the apartment, she felt a sense of relief, her body relaxing. She just needed time to breathe, time to make a plan, and, if she got a bus ticket to the nearby city, that would be a big help. Getting down to the city would be huge, just because it would be so much easier to disappear there. Vanessa was right about that. It would also quite likely be harder to get farther away. However, as long as Ania could get to the city and maybe find a job, that would help. At least she hoped so.

Did her father have a way of finding out if she got paid for work? If so, where could she work for cash, under the counter? Restaurants came to mind, but didn't they require a uniform? Maybe she could work in a laundry or as a night janitor. She pondered all these things well into the dawn, when she got a text message from her girlfriend, saying it was time to leave. Ania winced because that meant Vanessa was coming home. Ania got up, used the washroom, grabbed her purse, and waited in the trees outside, as Vanessa came home.

Vanessa casually checked the mailbox, just a collection of open bins, and dropped something inside, then disappeared into her apartment. As soon as she was inside the building, Ania waited for the next person to exit the lobby, giving her a moment to enter before the front door locked itself again. She checked Vanessa's mailbox and picked up the envelope and disappeared into the trees again. A note came with the bus ticket.

They came back. Twice. You'll have to watch it, and I don't know if you'll get onto the bus safely.

And, with that, Ania swore. If she couldn't get on the bus, she couldn't use the ticket. Not knowing what else she could do, she stayed put for a long moment, thinking over alternate options. Not wanting to bring any more pain to her childhood friends, Ania stepped out, feeling lost, and headed down to the main street. At the very least maybe she could hitch a ride from somebody going into the city. Not that it was the smartest thing to do, especially at nighttime, but she was out of options.

SANDERS AND RIFF had divided the small town into two sections, and both had spent the final daylight hours yesterday checking local businesses for Ania. They had decided to not go to the local authorities or even the hospitals, fearing her father would most likely do that. Sanders had no desire to run into him. Riff soon called off their foot search, due to darkness and to Sanders's lagging energy. The guys regrouped at the B&B and would start again first thing in the morning.

Early the next morning, after Sanders had stopped at several more locations, checking to see if anybody had seen Ania, Sanders walked into a café and ordered a coffee. As soon as it was ready, he took it outside and sat down on a nearby bench. He remained here for a moment, opening his mind and sending out messages, hoping that Ania would receive them.

When Riff walked up to him, he looked at him sideways. "Good idea," he said, pointing at the coffee.

Sanders nodded back toward the café behind him. "I just got it to go."

"Back in a minute." And, with that, Riff quickly bounded up the steps and entered the café.

Riff had so much more energy than Sanders, and he was envious, but he also knew that he didn't dare wait any longer at Terk's place before coming here and looking for Ania. Still, something strange in the energy was going on, and he couldn't figure out what it was. So, he pushed it, and he pushed himself. He was here trying to help somebody, and, even as he sat there, he knew that Cara and Clary were helping him more than they probably should be.

Clary sent him a message. *Stop. We are healers. We are helping you.*

He winced because, of course, everybody on Terk's team could read minds, and that was a hell of a thing. He replied,

We're not getting anywhere. Nobody's seen her.

Keep looking, she stated. *I don't know how or why, but I believe in you. I believe in the messages you're getting.*

Are you getting them too?

No, but energy is stirring on the ethers. I just don't know what that means for your situation. And, with that, she was gone again.

He was still contemplating her words when Riff exited the café, holding a cup of coffee of his own. He took one look at Sanders's face and asked, "What's that look for?"

"Just a message from Clary." He quickly filled him in.

"I agree with that," Riff replied. "I can feel the same energy moving. I just don't know what it's doing or who it's after."

"That's not helpful, and, so far, either nobody has seen her or nobody wants to talk."

"And yet, if she has family and friends here, that would make sense. People would protect Ania from all these strangers asking questions. According to Terk and the text I just got from him, Ania's aunt lives here and stays low under the radar. She's not terribly friendly with anybody."

"*Great,*" Sanders muttered, "so chances are, she won't talk to us."

"I wouldn't think so, but it's hard to say. We also have a couple friends of Ania's who are here. Then again, they may not talk either, as nobody knows who we are."

"Exactly. Nobody knows who we are. Nobody knows what we're up to or whose side we're on."

Riff shot him a hard look. "Yet you feel pretty strongly that there are sides?"

"Absolutely. Definitely there are sides. Nothing feels easy about this at all. I just don't know why I'm not getting in touch with her. The signals seem to bounce off."

"Maybe she's afraid that somebody's tracking her. Maybe she's afraid that messages are being received that aren't going where she wants them to go. Maybe she's afraid they are her father's goons, trying to trick her. Maybe she's not capable of sending them or receiving them."

"Yeah, it's that last one that's really worrying me," Sanders admitted. "I was amazed at her gifts. Yet how did she learn to use them? I don't know that anybody in her world has these abilities. We didn't discuss that."

"Why don't we go talk to the aunt? Maybe she'll let us know something."

Sanders grimaced. "You and I both know she won't though."

Riff laughed. "But it's important to feel as if we're doing something and to put that energy out there while we're at it, all in order to get somewhere," Riff explained. "We've come this far, so we'll try to stay positive."

With the address in hand, they quickly headed to the aunt's house. Once there, they walked up to the small 1940s house in the back of a larger home. No telling which one had been built first, but the smaller one had probably been servants' quarters or a rental at some time.

As they walked up to the smaller home, the door opened, and an older woman stepped out, her features hard as she snapped, "What do you want?"

That was the thing about Estonia, so many people spoke English. Not that it was a problem because Sanders knew quite a bit of Russian at this point anyway. Not that everybody spoke Russian either, but they managed to do pretty well when switching between languages. He dismissed the bruise on one side of her face and quickly explained that he was a friend of Ania's and that he'd come here on a surprise visit. However, so far, he hadn't found anybody who had seen her.

The aunt's gaze narrowed with suspicion. "She has no male friends. It wouldn't be allowed."

He studied her aunt and then slowly nodded. "We haven't met in person yet," he shared.

At that, she almost spat in his face. "Online? That's not a relationship."

He took a mental step back. "No, it's not," he admitted. "However, we can't have a relationship if I can't find her."

She crossed her arms over her chest, giving a stance of might, yet her fingers trembled.

Instinctively he added, "I wasn't sent here by her father."

Her gaze widened, and she turned, looking around in fear.

"He did not send us, and he does not know that we're here."

She shuddered. "You need to ensure he doesn't find out, or you can expect a bullet in your back," she muttered. "He will allow nobody close to her."

His breath went out in a *whoosh*. "Thank you for the warning. Would he also hurt her?"

She winced, still looking around again. "You need to leave," she whispered. "Just talking to you will put me in danger." And, with that, she slammed the door in his face.

He waited, hoping that she would come back out and talk to him. When she didn't, he left her a note in the mailbox at the side of the house. *If you get a chance, please let me know where she is, so I can help her.* And he left his phone number too. He didn't think that she would let him know, but he took that chance, and he wanted to leave her an av,enue if she did feel like she could do something.

He didn't know whether she was afraid of the father or the government or something else entirely. Yet, if she were afraid, she would likely lock down and do nothing. Victims had a hard time stepping out of their own victimology to help others. However, sometimes that was exactly the push that people needed in order to stop being a victim.

As they walked away, a young woman walked up to Sanders and asked in a low murmur, "Are you looking for Ania?"

He nodded. "I am," he replied, keeping his voice low but a smile on his face. "Nobody seems to have seen her."

"She just left this morning," the young woman shared, looking around nervously. "She wanted a bus ticket into the city, but her father has already been looking for her. He and his men kept coming to the bus station several times last night, where I work. I bought her a ticket, but then had to tell her it might be too risky to use it. She has to be extreme-ly careful."

Sanders nodded slowly. "Thank you for that. Do you think she's still in town?"

She shook her head. "No, I think she will hitch a ride, instead of taking the bus, so that her father wouldn't know."

He nodded, then turned to look at Riff, who was search-ing the area for clues or for those goons. "Does she have a phone now?" he asked her.

Immediately the woman shook her head. "Not that I know of, but she would be very careful with it if she did. Her father would never willingly allow her that much freedom."

He winced at that. "*Nice father.*"

"No," she countered, her tone harsh. "He's not, and, if he finds out you're looking for her, you better have a hell of a good reason, or he'll kill you."

He stared at her. "That's the second time we've been warned off."

"I'm warning you off, but I'm hoping you won't listen. Ania needs a friend who can help her right now."

"We're here to help, but I still must find her."

"That's the problem because she needed to get away, and she needed to get away fast." She turned to look back at the aunt's house. "Her aunt is too scared to do anything, so you should leave her alone. Plus, she is in danger too."

"I don't intend to cause her any trouble," Sanders said, his tone gentle. "I am here for Ania."

She studied him intently. When she relaxed a little bit, she nodded. "I don't know where she'll go, but she doesn't have much money, so she'll need a job right away. She won't take any legitimate job because her father will track her down that way."

Sanders winced at that.

The woman nodded. "So, look for dives, bars, and even worse, the streets," she shared. "I hope she doesn't have to go that route, but she'll need to eat, and she'll need to do something under the radar. She has her passport, so, if she can find a way to get out of the country, she needs to."

"You think her father will keep her locked up?"

"He's kept her drugged," she shared. "She didn't tell me very much, and some of it I could understand without being told, but she was on medication for antibiotics for an injury, and I think the antibiotics were something else. The people looking for her came to my booth at the bus station and told me that she's off her medications and had a rough reaction to one of them, and they're looking for her because they're so concerned about her health and well-being," she repeated sarcastically.

She shook her head. "The only thing they're concerned about is themselves. I just don't know why they care. Her father never gave a crap about her before her mom died, and, now that her mom is gone, he seems to be hunting Ania down, high and low. I don't like it," she declared bluntly. "And if you can do something to help, please do." And, with that, she was gone.

Riff moved closer. "Interesting," he murmured. "Ania has a few fans, at least."

"She has a few fans, but nobody's really capable of helping her."

"That's not true," Riff argued. "We're here."

With that, Sanders agreed. "I get it, but it's still pretty rough. Ania has no way of working properly, if her father will track her ID number."

"So, she'll get paid under the counter, but that's good because we'll follow her that way."

"Her friend didn't have anything helpful to give, did she?"

Riff's tone was slightly sardonic, as if that were standard. "I wonder if they ever do. Anytime somebody is in trouble, everybody knows they're in trouble. Still, no one knows how to help them and prefers that somebody else do the job."

"That's just typical of people," Sanders agreed. "Everybody wants to be safe, so they tend to not get involved." He looked around but still saw no sign of her. "She obviously knew what she was doing because she's long gone."

"Anybody who lives here is probably aware of Ania's plight or aware of what her father represents and what people coming and asking questions means for her," Riff explained calmly. "So basically everyone won't get involved, not if they know what's good for them."

"Right. In that case it's a good thing we have a little bit to go on, and, if she's managed to leave, she's headed into the city—probably looking for work and a way to get out of the country. So we have some idea *where* to look."

"She might want to leave the country, but her father will never let her go on her own. He will already have alerts set up at the airports and the seaports."

"Damn. I don't understand that," he muttered, as they got back into the vehicle. "Why would a father try to keep a grown, educated daughter under so much control?"

"I think that's the answer right there. … It's all about control. And, if he thinks that she has any special abilities, anything that'll make him money or will increase his status or power, you can bet he won't let her go."

"So, the biggest thing she has to do then is keep that detail away from him, so he doesn't know. Whether she can achieve that or not is a whole different story."

"Exactly. Let's head into the city and see if we can find her. Did you get a time frame on how far ahead she is?" Riff asked Sanders.

"Sounds like she left early this morning or even late last night, hearing word of her father and his goons watching the bus stop."

"So, she could be, at most, about fourteen hours ahead of us. That's long enough to disappear, if you know what you're doing. If you don't know what you're doing, it'll be a little harder. If she has some money, and she's not used to roughing it, she'll have to take some cheap accommodations, I would think."

"Which isn't really safe either, especially if she can't read people or use her telepathy."

They continued to hash it out as they drove into the city, which wasn't very far away. However, if Ania didn't have transportation, it was a far-enough walk to be an obstacle to her progress.

CHAPTER 3

I T WAS THE third place Ania had gone looking for work, and, as she waited nervously for the old man in front of her to answer her request, she shifted uneasily from foot to foot.

Finally he sighed and said, "I shouldn't."

She looked at him hopefully. "But you will?"

"It's bad. You should be home. You should not be here in this world," he replied, motioning around at the barrels that the employees were busily packing. "It would be day labor, hard work at that, and you'll be sore at the end of the day."

"Yeah, but maybe there'll be money to buy food," she added.

He winced at that. "The men, they will bug you."

She smiled. "I'm not worried about the men."

"You should be," he declared, glaring at her. "You're an innocent, and they will take advantage."

She hesitated and then nodded. "Thank you for the warning," she murmured, "but I still need to eat."

"I don't like it," he muttered. "You find a better job, you hear me?"

Her heart sank.

"But you can do that after today," he said, studying her. "You work here today. I'll pay you at the end of the day, and tomorrow you find something else."

She nodded slowly. "Thank you." She knew that he really was protecting her, didn't want her to be here, but was willing to give her a day's pay so she could eat. She almost felt bad about that because she did have a little bit of money. Yet she also knew that it wouldn't last very long.

He nodded and pointed. "I need the inventory on those shelves counted," he said, handing her a clipboard. "I don't like doing it anyway."

And, with that, she got to work. By the end of the day, she was sore, tired, and wondering just what the hell her world would be like from now on. However, that was a worry for another day.

The owner paid her in cash and repeated, "Don't come back tomorrow."

She nodded slowly. "Yet I didn't quite finish the inventory. I did get most of it done," she said, looking back at the shelving, "but you have those two racks left."

He stared at her. "Only those two racks?"

She nodded. "Yes, I've done the rest. Are you sure I can't come back just for tomorrow?" He glared at her, and she shrugged. "At least you're making good use of me," she shared, with a winning smile. "One more day is not a hard ask."

He groaned. "One more day, you finish the job, and that's it."

"Agreed." She smiled and thanked him.

He hesitated and then asked, "Where are you going now?"

She winced and shrugged. "To find a place to sleep." He glared at her again, and she nodded. "I get it, but the world is not kind when you're alone. And, when you're in trouble, it is even less hospitable."

At the word *trouble* he stiffened and glared at her, but she'd come to recognize the glare as a normal mannerism that didn't really reflect the person on the inside. "I'll be fine," she stated. "You've given me enough for food, and, if I can find a place to sleep for the night, I'll be okay."

"It's not safe to sleep on the streets."

"No, but some places I can go aren't very expensive." He again winced at that. "I just might not get too much sleep because of the noisy neighbors," she added, with a cheeky grin.

He chuckled. "You just be smart and don't take any clients yourself."

"I have no intention of that," she declared, smiling up at him. "Thank you."

And, with that, she took her leave, knowing that if she stayed a minute longer, she would probably get teary-eyed, and that would make them both uncomfortable. He was doing what he could allow himself to do, and she appreciated that. It was more than anybody else had done up to this point, so she could hardly judge him for not wanting to get involved, or for trying to send her off on her way to do something else. But she also knew that it would really eat at him if he saw her tears, since he was already worried that he was sending her away into a life of prostitution.

Definitely not in her plans. Neither had she wanted to use any of her energy for ill. She could if she needed to, but that wasn't the way she wanted her energy to work. She would eventually find a job and would work properly, without being afraid of turning around. Yet, if her father was still after her, that would be her life from now on, and anybody who helped her would have the same problem.

She also needed to add minutes to her secret phone but hesitated, as that was another expense. Plus, she'd used that phone to call her aunt, so it was possible her father could track her if she used the phone again. She had nobody to call at this point anyway. If she could call anybody, it would have been Sanders, but he was long gone, and she was grateful for that.

Sanders had been her father's pet research project, and that would never be easy. She'd spent considerable time trying to figure out how to rescue Sanders, and yet how does one do that when she couldn't even rescue herself? Thankfully, someone else managed to get Sanders free.

She shook her head and walked to the cheap hotel that she had found while searching for a job this morning. As she walked inside, the clerk eyed her, with a cheeky expression.

"Not going to feed yourself if you don't come home with clients," he muttered. "If you need to make a little money later tonight, just let me know."

"Thanks, but I'll be fine."

His eyebrows shot up. "You say that now," he pointed out a bit somberly. "Yet I've seen more than a few people start that way, but, mind you, it's not a sin to do what you need to do."

She stopped for a moment, realizing what he meant and nodded. "No, it certainly isn't. But, as long as I can find other ways to keep myself in food and housing, I'll try that first." She paid for one night's lodging, carefully counting out her cash.

"They all do," he cried out, as she went up the stairs. "They all do."

She tried to ignore him, but his words rang in her ears.

"It always ends up the same."

His warning was a daunting echo in her mind, as she flopped down on her bed. She'd picked up a little bit of takeout, mostly starches because she knew that would fill her the fastest. It wouldn't be easy being on the run. The clerk had been right. If she didn't find more work, it would be hard to keep this up. She also didn't want this as a life for herself. She needed to go to work in her own field, where she could make a real living, do what she had been trained to do. But she had to get out of this nightmare first, and, if she was living in a hotel, she also needed a phone that worked and couldn't be traced, as well as a laptop to search for jobs. Having neither at the moment, she would have to go to the library.

That was the only way that she could check out what was going on in the world and could find positions to apply for. Although she wasn't sure what she wanted, needed, or was in any shape to apply for work locally. Her father was likely to find her here, particularly when she had to start filling out the employment paperwork. She wouldn't put it past him to put a watch on her ID numbers, just to ensure that, if she did try to do something here, he would find out where she was. With a sigh, she realized that she had to move on. She had to leave this country—on foot, if need be.

That didn't mean he would instantly come in and grab her, but it didn't mean that he wouldn't either. Something was very daunting about a man who was prepared to tell people that she was completely incompetent, off her meds, and a danger to herself. His behavior had given her to wonder as to whether he truly was her father. Regardless, most people wouldn't go against him, and that was unfortunate because she didn't want to put them in danger. Still, she also didn't have the means or the wherewithal to get where she needed to go without help from others.

Closing her eyes, she sent out several more telepathic messages, hoping that somebody out there would pick one up. She was still dealing with a clouded memory, but, this time, it seemed that her signal was a little stronger. At least she hoped so. She tried again and then again, realizing that it was getting weaker as she went on. She would try again, as soon as she got a bit better at this.

Thankfully she had a job for tomorrow, which meant that she would stay here tomorrow night. Plus, she would have food tomorrow as well. It was all a matter of making the good things work for her and trying not to get overwhelmed by the ugliness of this life. With that thought, she quickly sat up, grabbed the takeout, and sat down to eat, chewing slowly, not sure when her next meal would be. By the time she was halfway through, she realized she had bought enough for later as well.

She put it off to the side, wondering how to get a new phone and whether she could even afford that. Her father had taken her first phone a long time ago, back when she had been sick. She'd asked for it later, and he'd refused to give it up. At that time, he'd managed to cut her off from her friends completely. She hadn't been allowed to go out with friends or to even visit the libraries. She did get a burner phone when she'd taken off for her aunt's, but that was already out of minutes, and Ania was worried about using it anyway. She got up and headed downstairs, where she asked the clerk if a library was around.

He nodded. "Yeah, sure, but it's not within walking distance. You would have to catch a bus."

She pondered that and then nodded. "Maybe tomorrow night then."

"Yes, maybe tomorrow night, but it's not likely you'll be any less tired then."

She glared at him. "No, but I'm trying."

He nodded again, but there wasn't any sympathy in his tone or his gaze. He'd seen it all before, and he'd seen too much of it.

She knew that he didn't expect her to survive this, at least on her current terms. She added, "I'll see how I feel tomorrow. Maybe I'll go there first."

"Maybe," he repeated. "Just remember you'll have to pay for another night tomorrow."

"I know," she replied steadily. "That's not the issue."

"Maybe not now," he said. "I just don't want to evict you if I don't have to."

She didn't say anything to that and headed back up to her room and had a shower. She sat on the edge of her bed, wondering what she could do when life had her in such a difficult position right now. She headed back downstairs and asked the clerk, "You know where I can get a cheap phone?"

He pondered that and asked, "How cheap?"

"Very cheap. My father took mine away."

He glared. "I really hate overbearing parents." He took a moment and then shook his head. "I've got an older one that still works."

"How much do you want for it?" she asked warily.

He laughed. "Not that much. I don't know, just a few dollars."

She nodded. "Then that would be great. Is it the kind I can add minutes to?"

"It is. I think some minutes are still on it. Don't you have a laptop?"

"I did, but my father took that away too," she shared.

"I'm feeling very cut off from the world."

"Yeah, that sucks, but I don't have a laptop for you. Sorry."

She nodded. "It won't be that easy to replace either. It's hardly something that those of us without money can afford."

"You can get used ones from the pawnshop a block down," he suggested.

"You mean stolen ones?" she asked, with a half smile.

"Do you care where it came from?" he challenged.

"At this point, no," she admitted. "I'm not a fool."

"Good. Go tell him that I sent you, and they'll see what they can do."

"But how much money is it likely to cost me? By the time I pay for the phone and keep enough minutes on it …"

He frowned. "Right. You can borrow my laptop for now," he stated, glancing around. "But it's not something I like to do."

"No, I'm sure you don't," she agreed. "The clientele here is not the easiest to trust, I presume."

"No, they aren't, and most of them would just as soon steal that laptop rather than bring it back to me. If that's the case with you, you'll be sorry."

And just enough threat filled his tone that she believed him. "I just need to connect with the world, to see what is out there for work, how I can get out of the country, and a few things like that," she shared, with a wave of her hand. "I'll even sit over here, if you want."

He brightened at that. "Yeah, that would be better for me. Internet is here in the lobby too." And, with that, he set her up at the small coffee table.

She logged on, feeling relief when she could catch up on

the news, her email, and send a few messages. She contacted her aunt, letting her know that she was safe but didn't say anything else—in case her father was tracking her aunt's emails too. Ania knew it made her sound as if she was obsessive and paranoid, but it was her father, and, when he wanted something, he didn't hold back.

No answer came from her aunt during the time that Ania was on the borrowed laptop, and she wouldn't necessarily get any answer down the road either.

When Ania found Vanessa's email, she quickly sent her a message too.

Almost immediately Vanessa emailed her back. *Two men were looking for you.*

Ania's heart froze, and she read the next line, just two words.

Call me.

Ania sent back an email reply. *No access to a safe working phone at the moment, but I hope to have one soon. I'm borrowing a laptop to catch up on the world.*

Her response came too quick. *The world's gone to hell, so you're better off if you don't catch up.*

Ania almost laughed at that but asked instead, *These men, what did they look like? Did they give you names?* When Vanessa's response came back, Ania smiled with relief when she read it.

The one looked like he cared about you, but he didn't give me a name, just said to tell you that he was safe. I don't know what that means.

Ania sighed. *He was safe.* She pondered that, realizing that the only person who would send a message like that would likely be Sanders. She sent another email message because she needed to know for sure. *What did he look like?*

She got a description instantly. *Both of them were over six feet. The one looked hard as hell, and the other one looked injured and recovering. They were both upset. They were almost resigned to hear that you weren't here.*

She pondered that, wondering if Sanders had come after her. The thought made her almost giddy with excitement because, if that were true, she wouldn't be quite so alone in fighting this nightmare, a nightmare she was acutely unprepared for. The emails went back and forth a couple more times, and then Vanessa got off with a warning, saying that she was deleting these emails, just in case.

No offense, but your father's one scary dude. I don't want to get on the wrong side of him. Meanwhile you need to get your ass out of here and get as far away as possible. I've got a new number too. With that last warning, Vanessa left her new cell number, along with a short postscript. *Your SM followers are over 1M! Check it out.*

Ania quickly wrote down Vanessa's new cell number in her notebook, then quickly hit her SM account. She shook her head at her massive number of followers. While she had her murderous, abusive father and his goons on the ground here, at least she had people online who renewed her faith in humanity. *It's not just me and Sanders against the world,* she thought to herself. She smiled broadly, as she returned the borrowed laptop to the clerk.

"Feel better?" he asked.

"Yes, thank you. A few calls for help, a little bit of assistance from a friend or two," she shared, feeling a lot better. "Checking up on email, all that good stuff. We're so connected now that, when you lose that connection, it's like you've lost your right arm."

He nodded. "You're not the first person to say that here.

I wonder if I should set up a little *rent a laptop for an hour* deal. It might be a good arrangement."

"You should," she agreed. "A lot of people here may not have a way of accessing emails and the internet without your help. It's a needed service you could offer."

He pondered that. "You gave it back in good condition, so that's good I guess." Then he held out a phone. "This is what I have."

She took the older flip phone and its charger from him, noting the phone still had bars and minutes. "Thank you. I'll go grab some money. How much did you decide on?"

"No, don't worry about it," And then he groaned. "I shouldn't even be doing this much, but seeing somebody who's trying to do something with their life and getting out of whatever trouble they're in, I feel you really need the help," he explained, giving her a smile. "The phone? … Whatever. It's not much, and, if you get a better one at some point, maybe you could return it."

She smiled, and this time it was genuine. "Thank you. Does everybody here realize what a con man you are?"

He looked at her. "A con man?" he asked, as if not sure how she meant it.

"Yeah, you come off miserable and gruff, but, inside, you've got a marshmallow for a heart." She could see that she'd surprised him, but he was also obviously pleased.

Leaning forward, he whispered, "Don't you go spreading that around. I have a reputation to maintain, you know."

She chuckled. "Oh, never. Your secret is safe with me."

With a bright laugh, she raced up to her room, feeling the best she had in several days.

EARLY IN THE morning, and once again armed with several of her photographs, Sanders and Riff split up and headed down through the rougher areas of the city. Sanders would hate to see Ania here. Yet, if she used her energy work to keep herself safe from various predators out there, she might find a job and somebody with a soft heart who would help her. Her energy and her aura was too good to not catch attention that way. He didn't know quite how she could use her energy, outside of that mind-reading, truth-saying part, but it was at least something that protected her.

He tried a few warehouses, went inside each shop down the street, even hitting delivery services, everywhere he could, using as much energy as he dared to burn through, trying to track her, even though he was a shitty tracker. Yet if he had any instincts that could lead him to her, it was worth trying. He needed to use them because Ania was a needle in a haystack.

It wasn't long before he realized his approach wasn't working. Hours later, he came to a hard stop outside a warehouse. The doors were open, and a lot of noise came from the inside, but it was all industrious, people busy working at whatever they were doing.

As he stopped, exhausted and almost panting from burning too much energy, an old man stepped out, gave him a hard look, and snapped, "What do you want?"

He smiled. "I'm trying to find a friend," he began. "She got on the wrong side of circumstances, and I'm hoping to find her, so I can help her." And he held up the picture.

There wasn't even a blip on the other man's features, but he took the time to study the photo and then shrugged. "No call for me to ever see somebody like that."

"No, probably not," Sanders conceded. "Yet her father is

after her and is intent on making her life very difficult because he's highly placed in the Russian government. He's kept her drugged and incapable of doing a whole lot for the last few months, ever since her mother died. Ania managed to escape, and I've found out she made it here into the city. But she can't work unless it's under the table, and I know that she's not in the best of health just because of the drugs that he'd kept her on. So I need to find her before he does."

At that, the other man's gaze sharpened, and he looked at him intently. "What is it you want with her?"

"We're friends," he replied instantly. "I was quite sick." Even at that, he reached up a hand to the sweat pouring off his face. "As you can tell, I'm still not in great shape, but I knew she was in trouble." Something nudged him to say more. "I've come to help her, if I can."

"Doesn't look as if you'll be of any help to anybody," the old man declared, his tone hard. "I hope you didn't come alone."

"Is there a reason why I need help?" Sanders asked, staring at the old man. "She's a good person, and, if she needs help, I would like to be there for her."

The old man sighed. "You're too late."

At that, Sanders stared at him. "What do you mean?"

"I told her not to come back tomorrow because I didn't want her stuck in this life."

"Stuck in what life?"

"This one," he said, with a wave of his hand. "She obviously has an education and skills. She worked for me for two days. You missed her. I just sent her home not long ago."

"Shit." Sanders pinched the bridge of his nose. "So damn close." Then he looked at the old man. "I don't suppose you saw which way she went or know anything about where she's been staying?"

He shook his head several times. "No. I don't know anything about her, outside of the fact that she needed money and talked me into keeping her on for a second day because she was doing such a good job. I would hire her full-time in a minute, except that it's obvious she won't stay. She needed a bolt-hole and some quick cash. She was here, but I knew she wouldn't be here tomorrow."

"Of course, and that's where you have to look after yourself and your business." Sanders stared aimlessly around. "I don't suppose … Did she say if she would go shopping or to the library or anything like that?"

The old guy looked at him. "Why would she go to the library?"

"I'm guessing she doesn't have a laptop or even her phone. Her father took it all away, and she surely hasn't had the opportunity to replace them yet," he suggested, pushing his hair back. "Two of us are out here looking for her, and now we have to start over."

"You found me," the old guy pointed out, "and she's not that much farther ahead of you."

"Maybe."

"Looks to me like you need to go crash though."

"I will when I know she's okay," Sanders replied, his tone determined. "In the meantime, I know her father's out here looking. He may send his goons, so please, if anyone else comes here, … please don't tell him what you just told me."

"Depending on who the hell he is and how he talks to me," the old guy replied, "it's likely I won't even know the language." With that, he gave a hard laugh and disappeared inside the warehouse.

Sanders dropped to a nearby bench, pulled out his phone, and contacted Riff. "Hey, she was here today. She worked in a warehouse for two days. He told her not to come back tomorrow because he figured she was in trouble and needed to get the hell out of here, instead of staying in this grubby lifestyle. He also mentioned how this warehouse of his was no place for a young woman." He quickly gave Riff the address of where he was.

Then Sanders continued. "He doesn't know where the hell she's gone either. When I asked if maybe she'd mentioned that she was going shopping or looking for a library, he thought that was an odd thing, until I explained she likely had no way to communicate. Still, he didn't know."

"Give me the coordinates for where you are, and we'll get Terk to hack into the city cameras and see if we can pick her up that way."

Brightening at that thought and worried that his own energy hadn't even allowed him to consider it, Sanders quickly gave Riff the address, then rose. "I'm heading your way," he added.

"Don't bother. Just stay where you are, and I'll come pick you up. You shouldn't be walking any more than you're already doing."

Sanders swore into the phone. "Yeah?" Yet he did sink onto the bench again.

"I can see the energy drain on your system," Riff muttered. "Wait until Clary gets a hold of you."

"Maybe," he replied in exhaustion. "But we were so damn close," he cried out in frustration.

"But the thing is, we're on her trail, and now we at least have some ideas to go on. Don't get upset. I'll be there in five." And, with that, Riff hung up the phone.

CHAPTER 4

T HE TRIP FROM the library back to the hotel hadn't been easy. The bus had broken down, and Ania had had to wait for another one to come. Then a rainstorm had blown through the area as she walked from the bus stop to her current lodging. So, by the time she got inside, she was trembling from the exhaustion of her day and from being wet and cold. She still had some food left, but it wouldn't be enough for tonight and tomorrow.

As she walked in, the clerk took one look at her and frowned. "You're dripping water all over the floor." Still, he waved her over and handed her a brown paper bag.

"What's this?" she asked.

"Some clothes left behind by a previous occupant. You can't keep wearing the same shirt and pants. Especially now that they are soaking wet."

She took the bag and nodded. "This is very nice of you. I'll be fine. I've got food up in my room. I'll go eat, and I might survive this."

He shook his head. "You shouldn't have to *survive* anything."

"I know that, but I gave up on fairy tales a long time ago."

And just enough bitterness filled her tone for him to sigh. "You're not the first person to say that either."

She gave him a look. "It really doesn't make me feel any better to know that I'm just following the path of other down-and-out but well-meaning people for the last God-only-knows how many years," she grumbled, as she trudged to the stairs.

"Take a cup of coffee with you," he called out.

She stopped and looked at him. "From where?"

He pointed to a cup that he had poured for her.

Such concern filled his expression that she felt a wave of gentleness wash over her. "Thank you." She backtracked and picked up the coffee carefully, so as not to spill a drop. "You're very kind. Trust me that I will enjoy this, after I get a shower."

"Enjoy it first," he suggested. "It won't stay hot that long."

Knowing he was right, she just nodded and climbed the stairs to her room. There, she sat down on the floor rather than getting the bed wet, from the rainstorm that had poured all over her. She sat here, with her eyes closed, trying desperately to hold back the tears. It hadn't seemed so bad the first day, but something about the second day and knowing that she wouldn't be allowed to return to her day gig had somehow made it even harder.

She could still show up there tomorrow, and maybe the warehouse owner would be nice and give her more work, but he'd made it pretty clear that he didn't want her back and that she should go out and get a better life. How the hell she was supposed to manage that was beyond her though. She'd also seen some hard looks from some of the other people working there today, and maybe that's what he'd been worried about. She certainly didn't need more trouble, yet, as she realized just how hard it was to do this, she felt sympathy for all the women who had taken this path before.

It was devastating. No support system, no money, no friends, nobody who could step in and help her. It all made her appreciate the plight for others in a way she never had before. What did women do? And, of course, the answer was clearly what had been intimated downstairs, and that was something Ania was determined *not* to do.

She had a bloody degree, for crying out loud, so surely she could find a job somewhere. She had to, because the other option was not acceptable. Not today or tomorrow, and, if it wasn't acceptable now, it wouldn't be acceptable in the future. Yet she also knew that, if she got to the point of being so broke that she couldn't eat or work, then pride might take a back seat, and she would do whatever it took to survive.

When this wave of absolute fury came at the thought, she had to laugh. "Okay, so much for that idea," she muttered. "Definitely not going in that direction."

With the coffee gone, she got up and had a hot shower. The hand-me-down clothes were actually in good shape and somewhat fit her. Her others were hanging on the shower rod, drying out. Feeling much better after that, she sat down with her cold dinner. No way to warm it up, although she probably could have gone downstairs and asked the clerk to do it, but she didn't want to impose any more than she had to. At one point in time, she was afraid a price tag would be attached, but, so far, she'd managed to keep herself free and clear of those kinds of consequences. However, she wasn't ready to push it and to take any chances.

Because she was so hungry, the cold food was just fine. By the time she was done, she had finished off the last bit of cold coffee and then curled up under a blanket, wondering if she dared go down and ask to use the laptop again. But she had his loaner phone, so, taking a chance, she quickly called Vanessa. When she answered, Ania spoke right off the bat. "Hey, I've managed to get a phone."

"That's a good thing."

"Any sign of my father?"

"No, but more goons are in the village now, so I'm pretty sure it won't be long before we see him too."

"*Great*, I'm so sorry."

"Don't be. He would be coming here, even if you hadn't seen me, and now I can just tell him that I saw you."

"Ouch, that won't go well."

"No, but he has no reason to get angry at me," Vanessa argued. "It's not as if he put out any alert to say it was illegal to help you, although I won't mention that."

Just enough humor in Vanessa's tone made Ania smile. "I'm really glad for the help that you did give me," she murmured. "I'm just starting to realize what life is like when you don't have any friends nearby, or a support system, or money, or a job."

"Yeah, it sucks," Vanessa agreed, "and that's why sometimes you just have to step up and help each other. I keep hoping that, by some miracle, there could be a day in the future when this is all behind you. Oh, by the way, I saw your aunt today."

"And?"

"She wouldn't even acknowledge me. She looked straight through me and raced on by."

"Crap. That just means she's terrified."

"Yeah, she's terrified all right, and had a busted lip to go along with her bruised cheek. She won't talk to anybody, be it friend or foe. I don't know whether it was your father hit her or one of his goons. Whatever happened between them, it's obvious she's running like a plucked chicken. If she had a place to go, I think she would be out of here as well."

"She has nowhere else to go …" Ania muttered. "That's where she and my mom grew up. In fact, she's living in the same house."

"So, chances are, she's as stuck as the rest of us," Vanessa replied glumly.

"Why? You didn't want to leave too, did you?" Ania asked. "If I had known that, you could have come with me."

"Yeah, sometimes I do envision leaving this place. Yet I thought I would be married by now, have a family, and not still be in my hometown. But, with no boyfriend in sight, no upcoming changes in my life, it's just the same old, same old."

"Yet you have a job, and that's a lot to be grateful for right now."

"Is it?" Vanessa asked. "I've saved up money, and I could probably go anywhere. However, it's not as if I have anybody who wants to prod me out of this rut," she teased. "I'm thankful that I'm not being hunted. Yet the craziness of the world out there scares me. Look at you and your aunt. I just don't really have any place to go."

"You could leave, you know."

"I could, if I really wanted to."

"I wish I had a place to go, but I don't. So I'm still stuck in the city."

"I don't even know how you managed to get out of here," Vanessa noted. "Will your father also be watching the airports and the major seaports?"

At that, Ania froze. "Good God, I don't know," she whispered, her voice catching in her throat.

"Sorry, I didn't mean to scare you."

"No, no, you may not have meant to, but it's a good thing you mentioned that because I hadn't even considered it. So I can't fly out from here or catch a ride on a cargo ship. I'll have to make my way farther on foot, I guess. Then maybe I can fly out from somewhere else."

"If you made your way to Europe or somewhere, you could probably risk a flight. You always wanted to go to Italy, didn't you? How about now?"

"Yeah, I would love to," she replied, with a laugh. "I have my passport, but what I don't have is any way to know how far my father's reach is. By the looks of it, I'm stuck with ground transportation that takes cash, for now."

After a few more minutes Ania ended the call, not knowing how many minutes were still available on her borrowed phone. She would have to keep tabs on that, saving some minutes for use in case of an emergency. Feeling a bit better, she went downstairs to return the coffee cup.

He motioned at the laptop and asked, "You want a few minutes?"

She grinned. "Absolutely I do. Thanks." She quickly took the laptop and sat down at the small coffee table in the lobby and checked in on the latest news.

Absolutely nothing appeared about her in the news, which was perfect, not that there should be. She couldn't imagine her father ever wanting to promote such public chaos or to put out a missing person's report on her. Yet, if it suited him and his purposes, he would do it in a heartbeat. So that was one of Ania's concerns.

After she'd spent a half hour online and sent off a few more emails, she headed up to her room with a *Thank you* to the clerk. She then curled up in bed, wondering what the hell she would do the next day. She would have to find another job, and that was starting to be the biggest thing in her world.

What she needed was to find another nice person, like the older man she had just done an inventory for, and see if they would give her a little bit of work for cash. As she started to drift off, she thought about Sanders, wondering if it really was him looking for her. She was rather desperate to believe it was. Yet it would be pretty easy to get it wrong. What if her father had utilized a sharp young man to make it look like somebody she might care about? Or at least somebody more pleasant than his usual goons, so people might respond better to their questions.

Her father would use a sledgehammer to get what he wanted, but he was smart enough to realize the time and the place mattered, and that just made him even more dangerous in this world.

Ania closed her eyes, exhausted, and fell into a deep sleep. When she woke up in the middle of the night, she heard her name being called out sharply. She bolted to her feet, staring around in a panic, and then whispered, "Who is it?" she cried out. "Who just called for me?"

Of course anybody else would think that Ania was nuts, and she didn't want to even think that her father might be right about that. That was the last thing she needed. No one answered. Still, she noted a weird buzz in her head. She dropped to the floor, closed her eyes, and sent out a telepathic appeal for help. *I don't know who you are or where you are, but, if you're there and if you can hear me, please let me know.*

More weird ringing came in her ears. She tried again and then once more. Finally, after half an hour of this crazy buzzing—almost as if somebody was tuning a ham radio—a voice came through. It was clear as a bell.

Ania, is that you?

"Yes," she cried out, bouncing to her feet and looking around the room. "Who is this?"

When the answer came, she couldn't hardly believe it. She let out a *whoop* and danced around the room. "Sanders, is that you? Is that really you?"

Yes, it's me.

SANDERS GRINNED, THE smile splitting his face from ear to ear, as he looked over at Riff. "I got her."

Riff turned and his eyebrows shot up. "Got her what?"

He tapped his head. "I just contacted her telepathically. She's here."

"Where is *here?*" Riff asked, walking closer. "Where can we get her?"

He closed his eyes, struggling with the reception. *Where are you? Let me know so we can come and get you.*

In a hotel.

What hotel?

And again the message was garbled. He frowned at that, looking over at Riff. "I'm getting really shitty reception here."

Riff shook his head. "You do know that there isn't great reception when drugs are involved, as in this case, yours and likely hers. Any drugging of Ania may be messing things up. If you tell me what telepathic wave she's on, I could join the conversation."

Sanders blinked at Riff, not understanding any part of what he'd asked.

Riff waved his hand. "Never mind. Just work on where she is, so we can go pick her up."

Sanders sent back another message. *Where are you? I need to find you.* He winced because she was screaming in his ear.

Sanders. Sanders! Where are you? Where are you?

And then came silence. He swore and looked over at Riff. "Whether it's drugs or not, I just lost her."

Fascinated, Riff half smiled and nodded. "This isn't like a phone communication. You won't just drop a call. That isn't how telepathy works."

Sanders stared at him, his lips twitching. "You may say that, but it's what it feels like right now."

"That's because something is going on between you guys, whether it's her end or yours. Whatever it is, some weakness is causing this disconnect. You need to deal with that, in order to reconnect with her."

"That's what I meant."

"*Uh-huh.*" Riff just shook his head and headed back to doing whatever he was doing. "Let me know if you reconnect."

Sanders remained in the same position for the next hour, trying to connect to Ania again.

Meanwhile, Riff was using his telepathy to connect with Terk, as he searched the ethers for hotel rooms, inns, and other places, looking for her, but all of that had been for naught. "According to Terk, we don't have anybody in the city registered as Ania, at least so far. They've got another couple hundred rooms for hire to check out," he added, with an eye roll. "Yet she won't be using her real name anywhere though. So chances are, she'll be at a dive where they really don't care, as long as she pays in cash."

"Right, and those are the first places we should be checking on foot, with her photo to prod their memory."

Riff nodded. "You just connect with her again. We need her to tell us more, and an address would be a great start."

That's what Sanders had been attempting to do. Finally he got up in frustration and grumbled, "It's just not working."

"I hate to tell you but you're trying too hard."

Sanders turned and frowned at him. "Didn't you just tell me to try?"

"I did, but I guess you don't have much training with this, do you?"

"No, I don't have *any* training at this at all. I tried to tell the bloody Russian government that, but they didn't care. They figured they had something special in me and didn't want to hear that I wasn't that special. *Special enough* was okay for those morons."

Riff's lips twitched at that. "You're definitely special," he replied, "and, with a little bit of training, you'll probably be damn wicked. However, at the moment, you're still sick and weak, and your system is fighting everything." His words may have been harsh, but his tone was nothing but kind. "So, that little bit that you're managing to do is pretty impressive."

"Huh?"

"Yeah. I would suggest you cut yourself some slack and realize that this is a huge breakthrough and that we will find her. We also have a tracker on the team, Langdon. He's searching for Ania, too, by her energy signature. So, right now, while everybody else is doing all their shit, I'll go crash. We need not *all* be exhausted." With that said, he got up and walked over to his bed and threw himself down.

As far as Sanders could see, Riff was asleep almost immediately. Yet Sanders knew that sleep would be completely impossible for him. What he could do though was lie down and send Ania messages of love and connection and joy. He felt confident that he could send these emotions, even if he couldn't speak telepathically with her. When she got these energies, they would let her know that she wasn't alone. Then maybe she could reconnect or could find that same vibration that they'd had before. Maybe she would recognize this transmission for what it was.

Sanders hated to admit it, but this was starting to sound a little sappily like real love, not just a connection with somebody who was in trouble. That's what he'd always chalked it up to before—just a connection between two people who maybe, just maybe, cared about each other. At least he hoped so. It would really suck if all the caring was just on his side.

CHAPTER 5

ANIA FELL ASLEEP again, waking to an odd sound that had her bolting out of bed and staring around her room nervously. She snatched the loaner phone off its charger and checked the time—5:00 a.m. She walked quickly to the window and peeked behind the curtain, not sure what was bothering her. It was not light outside at all, save for the streetlamps. Vehicles were parked up and down the road, as people had come home last night. With this hotel, vehicles for the guests were parked in the allotted parking lots.

Yet her instincts told her that something was wrong; she just didn't know what.

She quickly dressed, threw her few belongings into the one bag she had and stepped out of her room, knowing that nobody would care if she was here later today or not. She'd prepaid, and, if she came back, she would pay again. If she didn't come back—or couldn't—that was a whole different story. She raced down the hallway toward the rear stairs, taking them down to the exit.

Without warning, the back door opened in front of her, and there were two men, startled, but eyeing her, and then their features lit up in mild surprise. One wore a big fat grin, as he said, "Would you look at that? Just the person we're looking for."

She was snatched up, and all she could do was scream at

the top of her lungs. But, in this location, she highly doubted anybody would care. A hand was slapped over her mouth, and she immediately bit down hard on the nearest finger.

"You stupid bitch." His furious words were followed by a smack of his hand to her head.

But one man had loosened his hold, so, with her nails, she quickly scratched his face, while she kicked and punched, twisting and wiggling free, and was on the run immediately.

With the two men pounding the pavement behind her, she darted through back alleys, over fences, until she reached another parking lot and skittered under a van, getting road rash. There she holed up and waited, frozen. She was trying hard not to give away her position.

She heard footsteps thundering past the van, where she was lying. Then the men swore, one going left and one going right. She waited, her cheek flat against the concrete, as she desperately tried to regain her breath, not only that but she needed a plan, and again she needed a plan that would work. A voice broke through the fog in her brain.

Stay put. We're on the way.

She left out a soft sigh. *Sanders.* She closed her eyes, her breath raspy, as she whispered in her head, *Hurry. They found out where I've been staying, and I'm in a nearby parking lot, but I don't know where.*

Keep the signal on, he murmured. *We're in a vehicle, racing toward you.*

She wasn't even sure how that worked or what other abilities he had, but, holy crap, if he could come get her right now, he would be a lifesaver.

Did you see who it was?

She thought about it and could only give him brief descriptions. *Both six foot, the huge bodybuilder thuggish types.*

Black jeans, black T-shirts, not brush cuts but short hair, she replied. *Other than that, they looked like they'd been around the bend a few times, though I didn't have much of a chance to look. One's got fresh scratches on his cheek and the other one? Well, I bit his finger,* she shared. Then she almost laughed. *If they try it again, they'll get a lot more.*

Stay put, he repeated.

Oh, I'm staying put, but I don't know if they'll come back.

You let us know, but you stay where you are. We're coming to you.

Good, but hurry.

Do you have any idea of the address where you were staying?

She gave him the coordinates of the main cross-streets. *I don't know the exact address of the hotel though. It's not exactly prime living.*

No, and it doesn't matter whether it was or not. You stayed alive, and that's what counts.

Yeah, but I'm in danger of not being alive much longer if they find me. They're pretty mad.

Stay put, he repeated, a hard warning in his tone. *This is our chance to grab you. If we lose you now, … it'll be almost impossible to find you again. This time your father will lock you up for a life.*

The fact that he was correct didn't make it any easier to stay where she was, especially when she heard footsteps coming back. In her head, she sent out an alert. *They're back, looking for me.*

Don't move, just stay quiet. Stop sending the signal, just leave it on beat.

She wasn't even sure what the hell that meant, but considering that she was afraid somebody else might track it, she shut it down, knowing that the men had physical coordinates for the main part of the hotel, but she'd run quite a distance from there. With her eyes closed, she tried to disperse any energy around her, in case some energy worker was out there. She was just doing whatever she could, yet not knowing quite what she was doing, but desperately hoping that somebody would help.

Then another voice broke in, and he said, *I'm Terk. I work with Sanders. We're the ones who rescued him. You need to stop thinking. Just imagine calm, peaceful waves of cool energy spreading out from your body and away from these men. What you don't want to do is focus on them, and you don't want to* not *focus on them either. Just try to stay calm and keep that energy from being rattled.*

She froze. *Are you saying my father might have somebody who can track me?*

It's always possible. We have somebody who can track you too. So never assume that there isn't anybody else like us. What we have to do now is ensure my team gets there fast enough that you're not taken again. So, we need to ignore your father for now.

She agreed wholeheartedly but wasn't sure how to do it. *I couldn't give him an address.*

It's okay. While I've got a lock on your position, they're heading toward you. Also, we have somebody here that can give us further directions to a more accurate extent as well.

His calm demeanor was soothing her as well.

The biggest thing is for you to stay put. If you do get snatched, you keep this link open, I can track it. Stay with me now.

Somewhat relieved to hear that, but hating the idea that she might get snatched again, she closed her eyes and just focused on her breathing, anything to try and keep that sense of calm within her heart. To have it go sideways now would be the worst, so she tried very hard to remain calm. When she heard footsteps slowly walking around the parking lot, she felt the reactive tremors shuddering through her body, as she worked hard to keep everything from blowing up.

Then she heard the men's voices. "She couldn't have gotten far," roared one of the men. "What kind of fucking bitch is she?"

"Hey, we've got news from the tracker."

"Yeah, well, he's been wrong before. I don't know if he's just making up shit to keep us on our toes or what, but he's hardly a very good tracker."

"Maybe, but he told me that she's not far from here."

Her heart froze. It just boggled the mind to think that people were tracking her. But it could account to some degree on why she was struggling so much to send and receive messages. The men were talking again.

"Doesn't matter if she's fucking close or not. If she's not right here in front of us, it doesn't matter. It's just too far away. He needs to give us better instructions."

She heard phone calls and muffled voices, as they moved over to the street. She kept her own energy as calm and as quiet as she could, then Terk again whispered in her mind.

Stay still. Stay calm. You're doing just fine. When she heard another vehicle drive up and pull into the parking lot, Terk added, *That will be Sanders and Riff.*

She was almost giddy to hear it.

Get ready to go with them but not yet. I'm getting them closer to where you are.

A vehicle now pulled up beside her, and she froze again.

That's them. Stay calm.

She let out her breath slowly, and then suddenly someone was down on the pavement beside her. She cringed in shock and terror, only to see a man staring at her. The relief on his face was too serene to scare her. Then he flashed her a smile.

"Ania. I'm Sanders. You're a hard one to find. Come on. Let's get you into the vehicle and out of here."

With that, he quickly scooped her to his side, away from where the bad guys were and into the back seat of a car. He quickly pulled a blanket over her, and they calmly drove out and away.

"YOU CAN SIT up now," Sanders said, flipping back the blanket. He smiled down at the shock of black curly hair, pale white cheeks, and huge blue eyes blinking up at him. He grinned. "Even though I had photos of you, I can't say you are exactly how I expected you to look."

Her gaze narrowed, and she nodded. "Ditto. Albeit without the benefit of a photo." She slowly sat up and looked around. "Are they gone?"

"We drove past them getting out of the parking lot," said their driver.

She looked at him curiously and offered, "Hi, I'm Ania."

"Hi, Ania. I am Riff."

She turned back to Sanders. "Do you know somebody named Terk?"

He chuckled. "Sure do. Technically he's Riff's boss. He's the one who signed off on the mission that got me rescued. And this one too."

"I really appreciate the help," she murmured. "How many people are there like us who can do this?" she asked in wonder. "I mean, all of a sudden, something that we thought was very unique and not widespread seems to be what everybody wants. More and more people can track us too."

"I think that's because they suddenly see a purpose behind our gifts," Sanders explained, as he looked around the street, his gaze coming back to her. "Of course we also know that your father is very involved in trying to supply more of us."

She winced at that. "My father has a lot to answer for," she declared, her tone harsh.

"Yes, just not today," Riff added.

Sanders let out a sigh. "I hate to tell you, but you should hear it from me. Your aunt is dead."

Ania gasped, a hand going to her mouth.

"We figured your father was to blame."

She nodded. "My mother was ill, but she was not on her deathbed. So I'm afraid he may have killed my mother too. Oh, Vanessa," she exclaimed.

"Terk has her in a safe place. He had another man in the area, so he'll watch over Vanessa, until we have your father under control. We're more concerned about getting you out of here than making him pay for anything."

"Can you get me out of here?" she asked, staring at him.

"We can. At least that's the plan," he noted. "We just need a little bit of cooperation."

"From whom, though?" she murmured. "Because, when you think about it, I do have a passport, but my father's got to be looking for me at all the major airports and seaports and other terminals," she shared. "I don't know how to get out of the country."

"We can drive, so that would be one avenue. I doubt he'll check all the roads."

"Unless he declares you some criminal and engages the local authorities to put up roadblocks," Riff commented.

Ania snorted. Riff was right. "He would do that in a heartbeat, if he thought it would get him what he wanted." Riff looked at her in the rearview mirror, as if checking the veracity of her comment, and she nodded. "He's changed since my mother died," she murmured. "My mother always kept me somewhat protected from him. Mostly I think because he was quick to use his hands to hit her. She always got the backhand but tried to keep me clear of it. Until recently, I was attending university in town, while he required me to still live at home. As long as he didn't know about what I could do, I lived a relatively peaceful life. But my mother knew that I had some abilities and didn't want him to find out. … I don't know what happened after she died. I don't know whether she left him a note or somebody mentioned something, but, all of a sudden, he was all over me." She turned to look again at Sanders. "I was being held, the same as Sanders was, but in a different way," she murmured. "I was under house arrest, whereas you were in prison."

"A prison that was a lab," he muttered.

Her face winced at that. "I am sorry. We don't really realize what we're capable of, until we get in these situations, do we?"

"In your father's case, I think he was scared about handing over people who supposedly had special gifts. So he was big on testing us, and, of course, I never quite got the testing right," he shared, with a waggle of his eyebrows.

She beamed. "Yeah, I never did either. Not that he really understood what we could or couldn't do, and I think that's been our salvation. So far, he doesn't really understand what we are capable of, so it's been a little easier to hide. But those men back at the parking lot, they did say that they were speaking with a tracker. Although they were complaining that their tracker wasn't good enough."

"A tracker?" Sanders repeated, slowly letting out his breath.

Riff nodded. "A good tracker is worth his weight in gold. However, if you're no good at tracking, that just makes it even harder, almost impossible, in fact. Add in some wrong information and a few missed signs a couple times, then nobody'll believe you."

"Their tracker did tell the goons that I was close, and they were standing right beside me. I was under that vehicle, hoping that they wouldn't bend down and see me. That's when Terk told me to stay calm and to disperse my energy, not thinking about what was going on because just thinking about them could bring me to their attention."

"Yeah, that can happen," Riff agreed. "The minute you activate energy, it has its own pulse, a unique beat. So, if you try *not* to think about something, … it's likely guaranteed that you'll think about it. As soon as you do, you get that weird feeling of somebody looking at you. You turn around, but nobody is there, and they get that same feeling. Of course, in this case, it just means that they would have turned around and would have doubled their efforts to find you even faster."

"That's insane." Anai was skeptical.

Sanders added, "The fact that we left and that they didn't find you is huge because you are free and clear of the men on the ground. Now the tracker is a worrisome loose end. So it's a matter of getting you farther away," he murmured. "For that, we'll have to work a little harder. First off though, are you hurt?"

"No, just scraped up a little."

"Do you need anything? When did you eat last? Are you okay for a long trip?"

"I had leftovers last night, but I was so keyed up that I couldn't really eat. Then I had a lot of trouble getting to sleep. Yet I slept like a log for a while but woke up with my heart slamming against my chest, knowing something was wrong. I just packed up and bolted outside, and they basically caught me leaving at the back door. I screamed bloody murder, fought like crazy, managed to slip free, and just ran. I was exhausted by the time I hit the next parking lot. When I thought I was out of sight for a second, I just dove under that van and stayed there."

"That was a great decision. Most people look high or on the ground, but to check under every vehicle wouldn't necessarily have been considered. That was good thinking on your part."

She smiled. "I would like to say I thought it through that much, but really I just saw a chance and went for it." She yawned, sitting up again. "I have to admit that this has been a pretty rough week."

"It has been," Sanders agreed. "We tracked you down to the old guy who hired you to do inventory."

She stared at him, her jaw dropping. "What?" she cried out. "You were that close, and I didn't know?"

He laughed. "We were that close and were trying hard to get closer, but you were on the move. So trying to follow you was like trying to find an ant in the dirt. Sure, you went to a big city, where you would blend in more, but it also made it harder for us to find you."

"I didn't even think about a rescue," she shared. "Plus

my father had kept me fairly drugged. So every time I tried to send out messages, I seemed to be working with a very low-powered battery. I was getting really fuzzy signals."

"You would have been," Riff confirmed. "It's a thing for Sanders here too, since he's still damaged from everything that happened to him. He's getting help from other people, sharing their energy with him to keep him strong and active—which he shouldn't be burning through, since it's other people's energy." Riff shot him a glare.

At that, Sanders nodded. "I understand, but I needed their energy to find Ania, and now that we have, I should shut it down—providing we don't lose her again."

"Don't lose me again," she whispered. "Please don't lose me again."

He reached out his hand, and she gripped it. "I don't plan on it," he stated. "You were what kept me sane that whole time I was a prisoner."

"I don't know about keeping you sane, but I was trying to figure out what I, or anybody, could even do for us," she noted. "I mean, we were both prisoners, just in different ways. I never told you very much about it though."

"No, but I understood," Sanders said. "You weren't free to help, and I didn't expect you to."

"And yet I should have," she admitted. "I was told that the pills my father gave me were antibiotics—because I had a bad cut on my arm, bad enough that I needed stitches. So I never thought anything of the pills."

"Exactly. And that's the thing about drugs. They keep you in that state. Once that first drug goes down, it's hard to know that you're being fed more lies and more drugs, so that you can't ever quite get clear," Sanders explained. "How did you finally figure it out?"

"I think I grew a little more resistant to the drugs," she guessed, with a wince. "I started to get a bit clearer and realized something ugly was going on. My father wouldn't talk to me about it, and then I realized that he was changing my drugs, adding medications, switching drugs, even though the wound had healed. I finally realized what was happening, but getting away from him was a whole different story. Once I knew that Sanders here was free and clear, then it gave me hope that maybe I could get out. Obviously I was hoping that he would come after me someday, but I didn't really see any way for that to happen. So I didn't hold out much hope for it."

Sanders sighed at that. "It hurts to hear that, but I get it. When you're a prisoner, you hang on to every little bit of hope that's possible, and I get why you would also think that maybe I couldn't come, but, hey, we got you out anyway."

She squeezed his fingers. "Thank you."

Sanders asked, "So you didn't tell us if you needed anything."

Ania smiled. "Can I get to a bathroom, get some coffee, maybe some food? If not, it's okay, but—"

"Absolutely," Riff replied. "Let me get an idea of where we are and where we can go from here. We need to stop and check in with the others anyway," he added, taking a look around. "It's just a matter of staying safe at this point."

"Staying safe is one thing. Staying away from my father, who's got eyes and ears everywhere because he's big in the military and the government—is a whole different story."

"Got it," Riff said. "Still, we're not really into failing. So stay strong, give us a chance, and let's get you into a washroom, a hotel, or at least a coffee shop, where we can connect with a few of our people." Saying that, he pulled into a truck stop up ahead, then looked around and asked, "You want to chance going in?"

She nodded. "I have to use the bathroom, so I have to go inside, unless one is outside." She sighed. "I would love to go in and sit down and have a meal, but—"

"Exactly. We won't take a chance on that. Sanders will take you in to use the bathroom and then order some food, while I check in with the team."

And that's what they did. By the time Sanders escorted her back to the car, he looked down at her, ensuring she was comfortable. "You feel better?"

"A little bit, yeah," she said. "Nothing quite like knowing that you're out of an ugly situation, even though it's still dicey. Obviously I'm ecstatic just to be free."

He gave her hand a squeeze.

"But the fear is still there," she admitted. "Now that my father killed my aunt, I also think he killed my mother."

"We think so too. In fact, I'm guessing that Riff is doing his own side investigation into that each time he disappears. So that fear is healthy in that it keeps you alert. I'm glad to see that. We have to be realistic about our situation. I came back for you as soon as I was able. Ever since I got back, we've been trying to catch up with you, but you've been staying under the radar pretty well."

She chuckled. "I had to. My father is not exactly slow on the uptake. When he decides he wants something, he goes after it, whether you like it or not."

"He's your blood father?"

She looked up, smiled, and nodded. "Yes but I have wondered about that. However, if you're thinking that's not normal behavior for a father, you also have to understand his motivations. He's extremely loyal to his country, Russia, and he loves money, but mostly it's power that does it for him. And handing over someone, a blood relative no less, who has all these abilities that somebody in the government says they need, would give him incredible power and a step up. That leverage is worth so much, within the government, the military, and elsewhere," she noted. "So, I understand his point of view and why he's more than happy to hand me over. I'm just not very impressed that he was totally okay to do it against my will."

"Right. Because you are still a prisoner because it's not your choice."

She nodded.

He got her settled back in the car. "It would be best for you to stay out of sight."

"I'm fine with that. I just want …" When she hesitated, he seemed to want to know more, and she shrugged. "I'm just scared to be alone, in case they return."

"I'm staying here with you, so no worries there. I'll pick up the order when it's ready, but, other than that, we'll sit here and wait for Riff to come back."

"Any idea where he went?"

"To make a phone call or two, I presume." Sanders looked around, but he himself wasn't exactly sure what Riff was up to. Sanders saw no sign of the man. It wasn't a problem, until at least ten minutes had gone by, and Riff didn't return. That made Sanders uneasy. He needed to go in and get the food, but he was unwilling to leave her outside alone. So, he sent out a message to Terk. *Have you heard from Riff?*

Terk's reply was instantaneous. *Yes, there's a problem. You have to take over the driving.*

That's fine. I can drive. I need to go pick up the food and the coffee I ordered, but Riff was supposed to be watching her while I did that. He set out to contact you, and there hasn't been any sign of him since.

Hang on.

Sanders tried to give her a reassuring look. "Come on. Let's go pick up our takeout order, and then we'll hit the road."

She scrambled out of the back seat, and he led the way into the restaurant. They quickly paid for the food, then went back to the car. She got into the front seat this time with the food, and he got in on the driver's side. Mentally he sent out a message. *Terk, where is he?*

Riff's gone to cover your tracks. He's also picked up a tracker's energy—not one of ours. You guys drive out of there fast and right now.

And, with that, Sanders slammed the vehicle into gear and pulled out of the parking lot and headed down the highway at top speed.

Ania frowned at him. "What happened?"

He gave her a smile. "Let's just say, our plan has changed."

CHAPTER 6

A NIA LISTENED TO the sparse explanation Sanders gave. "I feel bad leaving Riff behind."

"I do too, but, one thing I know for sure is, Riff is quite capable of looking after himself. He has a way of making things work out."

"Maybe, but I would have thought the same thing about myself. The lesson I've learned here lately is that everybody needs help sometimes."

"If we learn that Riff needs help, we'll be there to give it to him," Sanders stated. "But first we have to get you away from here, and that means moving fast. Riff's on his way, and we'll pick him up somewhere else." After a moment, Sanders looked over at her and said, "I could really use some of that coffee."

With a startled exclamation, she nodded and put one in the cup holder between them. "That's yours. We'll keep Riff's here, in case we pick him up soon."

Sanders nodded but didn't say anything.

"Do you think it's okay if I eat without waiting for him?" Ania asked.

"The reality is, it could be days before we pick him up," Sanders shared, his tone steady. "So you eat whenever you are hungry, and I would say, sooner is better." His gaze kept going to the rearview mirror.

"I gather we're in trouble," she noted hesitantly.

"My orders were to drive us out of there and quickly. Terk asked me not to wait for Riff, so I'm not sure that we're in trouble, as much as we needed to get down the road so we can avoid trouble."

"Avoiding trouble sounds good to me," she muttered.

He laughed. "Anytime we can get out of a scenario safely, we're all for it."

She nodded. "I know that it wasn't just your doing, and, given the choice, you would probably be somewhere far away from where you are right now," she shared, feeling quite emotional, "but I have to tell you how much I appreciate the fact that you came back for me."

He frowned at her. "Are you kidding? Of course I came back for you, and I will always come back for you. You were the only one who kept me sane for a long time. Once I realized that I would make it, I knew I was coming back for you, come hell or high water. However, it took me a little while to regain my strength, and I am not anywhere close to there yet," he added, with a nod. "So, if you see me getting really tired, that could become an issue. Regardless I wouldn't leave you alone to suffer like that. I wasn't sure exactly what your scenario was, but the last thing I remember was something about your father being behind it."

"Yeah, I probably told you that in a weak moment," she admitted, with a laugh. "I'm not used to talking about my problems."

"I understand. Yet, when you're a prisoner, and it's dark and lonely, and we can only talk through our minds," he explained, "it's very normal to reach out and to talk to somebody about circumstances which were horrific for all of us. I didn't think I would ever get out of there, so connecting with you made it a lot more bearable."

"Do you have any idea how long you were a prisoner?"

"At least six months," he estimated, "but I'm not sure beyond that because I'm not certain when I was snatched, especially after being pumped up with drugs. The last thing I remember is being in a movie theater, where I met a bunch of friends." He stared ahead, taking a moment. "Then it all just blew up in my face."

"Right. That would be my father. He has a tendency to do things like that. He must have found out that you had some ability, then had you picked up out of the blue, leaving you with no idea what happened."

"Exactly. I don't even know whether it happened that night or it was later, but that is the last memory I have, before I was kidnapped," he shared, with a shrug. "When you realize something like that can happen, and you can't even think rationally anymore, you just react. So don't ever apologize or worry about us going out of our way to help you," Sanders said. "We would help anybody in a situation like that."

"Oh."

At that, he winced. "That didn't come out right. I didn't mean to make it sound as if you weren't special because you are," he clarified, quickly trying to correct himself. "You are very special to me. I know I'm making a mess of this, but I don't want you thinking we would have done this for anybody, yet obviously we would have done this for anybody." Then he stopped again, confused, not sure how to undo what he had just implied, while trying to explain.

She burst out laughing. "In other words, I'm special, but you still would help ordinary people too."

"Exactly. Wow, you spelled that out much better than I

did. Maybe I'm more tired than I thought."

"Maybe you shouldn't be driving," she suggested, eyeing him intently. "I am so glad to see you, but I don't want to escape my father's goons just to die in a car crash."

"That won't happen," he said, "but, if my energy drops too much lower, we may have to find a place to hide so I can rest."

"Or I could drive," she offered.

He frowned at her, and she laughed. "Yes, I can drive—and very well, thank you—but I would need to know our destination."

"How about you hand me one of those sandwiches," he replied. "That will give me some energy to keep going for a while."

"Food," she muttered, directing her gaze to the large bag they'd grabbed from the waitress. "How much did you order anyway?" she asked, as she opened it up and saw multiple sandwiches.

"Lots," he stated, with a smile. "I didn't know how long it would be between stops, and we didn't get breakfast." He shrugged. "Besides, I'm a big eater, and Riff has a whole thing for food too. I needed something I could keep eating throughout the day, particularly at times when my energy is pretty nonexistent."

"Makes sense to me," she murmured, as she handed him a sandwich, partially unwrapped, so he could just hold it and take a bite.

For the next ten minutes, they both dug into the food and the coffee, enjoying the sustenance. By the time he was done with his sandwich, he picked up his coffee again and sipped several times. "It's almost calm enough to make me feel as if everything is nice and rosy again."

"*Almost*," she noted. "It's pretty upsetting when I think about it, though."

"That's why you don't dwell on it," he declared. "Your father will still be there to deal with down the road, but, at this moment, we don't have to deal with him. He can wait."

She chuckled. "I'm glad if that Pollyanna attitude has gotten you a long way in life."

"It has, to some degree," he confirmed, "but maybe not as far as I may have hoped."

"So, maybe you need to tell me a little bit about your life and about yourself."

"You mean, more than we already talked about?" he asked.

She shrugged. "It seems different now that you're right here beside me."

"It is, in a way," he agreed. "I was in the US Navy for many years and went into secret ops. Then I was badly injured in an accident. After that, I had many surgeries and spent quite a few years in rehab, just trying to rebuild my life. It's been quite a struggle since then. But how do you rebuild a life that is so opposite to what you had always felt was destined for you? Talk about a fish out of water. I went from one job to another, trying to figure out what I wanted to do. I considered going back to school. Anyway I was bumming around with some friends, who had come into town, then *boom*. I was kidnapped."

She looked at him, puzzled. "But how would my father have discovered that you had any skills in the first place? That's the part that doesn't make any sense to me."

"I've wondered about that a lot," he admitted, "because there really wasn't any reason for it. I had been joking with some friends because I had done some work, some testing in the navy, looking to join a couple different teams working on some Cold War programs. I was wondering if it was worth even trying something like that again. Maybe that's how your father found out.

"Not that my friends sold me out, but that your father may have been spying on these programs and their participants. It's not out of the realm of possibility that maybe some tester in the program told him how I had been part of it, how I had performed well or whatever. I don't know," he said, with a headshake.

"It was quite a shock to wake up and to find out I was a prisoner and being tested for my psychic skills. Plus, I needed to protect myself—physically, mentally, emotionally, psychically—so that was tough because I didn't have any skills yet, not in regard to my gifts. It wasn't the field that I was working in, or anything I necessarily wanted to do, so I hadn't pursued it. All I know is that it's just what I ended up doing," he muttered.

"Did you ever give him any positive results?"

"Not really. I tried to make it all as confusing as possible, which was easy because I was confused about my so-called gifts," he replied, with a laugh. "I figured that, if he got even a little bit of positive feedback, it would make him all the more excited. Then he would just push me for more and more and more. So I balked. I underperformed."

"Exactly. My father and his goons would have done just that," she stated, with a nod. "Smart of you to figure that out early on."

"Hey, I was a prisoner, and I was looking to find a way to get the hell out of there. But I was kept locked up underground, and that was starting to weigh me down," he muttered. "It's hard to forgive their harsh treatment. We, as a species, need sunshine and fresh air and food and water and even someone to talk to, and when all of that is taken away, you don't forget, and you just fight harder and harder because the only other option is to give up. Yet, when you do that, it's permanent."

She nodded. "I hadn't gotten to that point and was still trying to figure out how serious my father was about all of this and how he even found out that I had any abilities to begin with. After my father found my journal, he was quite livid, stating he had burned the *vile creation*. I can only think that there must have been a journal in my mother's things as well. that he went through after she was gone. Even that he *read* her journal is surprising because I normally would have expected him to just toss her things out as trash. He didn't seem to care about her anyway, but it's all still a mystery at this point."

"Maybe it's better to leave it a mystery for now," he murmured. "We can't get carried away or have anyone question it and get into trouble themselves. It's just better to wait and see what turns up."

"He doesn't take to questioning, by the way," she shared. "He's a bully and a hardhead on top of all his power-mad craziness."

"Sounds like it," Sanders muttered. "The thing is, everybody has something they want. In your father's case, obviously it was more power, and he thought using our gifts was a way to get it for him. The flip side is also the crux of our problem right now because, if having us under his control could increase his access to power and could put a feather in his cap, losing us will make him lose badly, especially if he's overinflated our potential usefulness."

"And you can bet that some people have already been

punished for losing us," Ania pointed out. "However, we can't help that because, when you're fighting for your life, you don't have the luxury of compassion for whoever else gets hurt, particularly if they were among your jailors."

"You can't care," he agreed. "That's the problem. You can't care, and you shouldn't feel bad about it. Once you get to this point, it's an ongoing fight for your life and your freedom. As soon as you're in a fight with stakes that high, you can't consider anything but how to get out. Once it's become a life-and-death deal, it no longer matters who else gets hurt."

"Except for my mother and my aunt," she muttered.

"Hey, you can't feel guilty about what your father did."

"Yet it shouldn't ever have come to that, where innocent people are killed, even people in his own family," she cried out softly.

They talked for a few more minutes. As they drove along, she appeared to relax and let go a bit.

Smiling, he suggested, "You should get some sleep, right?"

"No, my job is to keep you awake," she declared, "so that'll hardly work." But, since they'd eaten, she had been yawning with some frequency.

"I'm fine for now," Sanders noted. "Go ahead and get some sleep. It's better that you get some rest now, in case I do get too tired. Go ahead and sleep, so I can call on you to take over later."

She straightened up and frowned at him.

He chuckled. "I'm fine, but we don't know what'll happen next, so best you get some rest while you can."

She nodded. "Are you sure?"

"I'm very sure. Go ahead, get some sleep."

And, with that assurance, she curled up against the door and whispered, "You'll wake me if anything goes wrong, right?"

He laughed. "We're both in the same car. Trust me that you will know."

With that, she smiled, closed her eyes, and very quickly drifted off.

He watched her slip into a deep sleep at his side and smiled. She was doing so well. Everything she'd been through—the loss of her mother, her father drugging her to control her, then the loss of her aunt, the stress, the drugs, all the running, and fear of not having a roof over her head—it was too much.

As Sanders saw it, the last few days had to be catching up with her, and it would take more than a few days to recover. That's what happened when people did shit like this, and Sanders could only imagine how much worse it was for her, knowing her own father was taking away the people in Ania's life, trying so hard to exploit her abilities and to essentially imprison her for life.

The stress was unimaginable, and it would take a while for it to finally ease back and for her to realize that she was safe again. In her case, it would probably take a lot longer, since it involved her father, who seemed to have a long reach. Ania would always be looking over her shoulder, especially until they got her out of the country. Sanders was still waiting for instructions on how to make that happen, but he was driving and would continue to drive as long as required to keep them both safe. They needed to stay ahead of the trouble because he was under no illusion where her father was concerned.

If her father found out that Sanders was here and had

been instrumental in Ania's rescue, Sanders expected there would be hell to pay in more ways than he was prepared to think about. It also raised the stakes in terms of their recapture in so many ways, since her father would dearly love to have not just Ania but the both of them, back under his control. That was something Sanders wasn't prepared to let happen and would do whatever it took to prevent it.

When his phone buzzed about an hour later, he pulled over to the shoulder, reached for his cell, and quickly answered. "Riff, is that you?" he asked.

"Yeah, it's me," he murmured, sounding tired. "Take down this address. Head there, and I'll meet you in the morning."

"How far away is it?"

"About a six-hour drive."

Sanders winced at that. "Okay," he muttered. "We'll make it. Are you okay?"

"Yeah, … I'm fine. I'm—I'm fine. Tired, but that's all right. I'll make it."

Once the call ended, Sanders punched in the address to his GPS, confirming they were six hours away easily, if not seven. He returned to the roadway and picked up his speed and opened the window, letting the vehicle run as hard and as fast as he could. The only thing that would hold him back tonight would be gas, so he checked the tank and would continue to do so. With their vehicle being stolen, he had no idea if it was a top-heavy tank reading or not.

Still, he would get as far as he could and then find a place to gas up. Hopefully she would sleep until then. With the window open and the coffee in his hand, he faced the highway and let the miles run.

CHAPTER 7

ANIA WOKE UP in the front seat of the car, stiff and sore. When she turned, Sanders smiled at her from the driver's seat. "Hey," she greeted him, her tone gritty. "I guess I really slept, *huh?*"

Sanders chuckled. "You went out pretty fast."

"I didn't think I would," she murmured, as she straightened up and stretched. "Where are we?"

He quickly pointed out their location on the GPS map on his phone. "This is where we're headed." He again pointed to his cell.

"Oh, did you hear from somebody?"

"I did. We're meeting Riff there."

"Oh, thank heavens for that," she cried out in relief. At his look of surprise, she shrugged. "I wasn't sure that he was okay."

"He's fine, and he has a plan to get you out of the country. I don't know the details or even much about where we're headed, but I trust Riff, so let's hope it works."

"Yeah, our destination is right along the southern border," she noted, "so in a way it's a good choice, as long as we can get across into Latvia, without drawing too much attention to ourselves."

"That's the plan," he said comfortably. "I've put my trust in these men so far, and I'm not about to doubt them now."

"I hear you there." She yawned and asked, "It'll still be a few hours, right?"

"Yes, and I need to hit a gas station soon. Looks like one is about two miles away."

"Good, if we can stop, get gas, fresh coffee, and a pit stop for my bladder," she shared, "I would really appreciate it."

"No problem, and good timing anyway."

The signs for the gas station came up soon afterward. He pulled the vehicle into the station, quickly started to fill up with fuel, then turned to her. "Wait for me, and I'll take you to the bathroom." She hesitated, as if not sure what to say, but he cut her off. "No, you wait."

"What if somebody comes and steals the car while we're gone?" she asked, with a note of humor.

"Then I'll steal another one," he stated, his tone serious. Her eyebrows shot up, and he nodded. "Believe me that this is not something to fool around with."

"Right," she said, now frowning.

Once he had paid for the gas, he followed her to the bathroom, and, after she'd used the outside bathroom, he took his turn, with her promising to stay right beside the door.

When he came out, she smiled at the look of relief on his face when he saw her. "I said I would stay here."

"You did, but that doesn't mean that somebody else would try to take away your ability to do so."

She winced at that. "Thanks for that reminder, though I can't say that's something I really want to think about too much."

"Maybe not, but let's go grab some hot coffee really

quick. Then we'll hit the road again."

With fresh coffee in their hands, they piled back into the car and took off. "By the way, where did you get this car?"

"I have no idea," Sanders replied. "Riff got it."

She burst out laughing. "Okay, so I guess I shouldn't ask questions I don't really want to know the answers to then, should I?"

"No, you shouldn't," he teased, "but I understand why you would ask. I sure didn't think to ask, and I'm just surprised you didn't ask before this."

"Me too." She was still chuckling, as she looked over at him. "But, hey, it seems Riff's got his head together."

"Oh, he does, indeed," he said, with a smile. "His team members are all very capable."

"Do you know much about Terk?"

"I know a lot about him. I started staying with them after I was rescued, just because I needed so much healing," he began. "I'm also interested in working with them, and they're interested in hiring me, so that will be good."

"Doing what?" she asked.

"Similar to what I'm doing for you," he replied. "Rescuing people, search and retrieval, deep research in some cases. Basically developing my abilities so I can be more of a team participant than I am right now."

"To even think that such a team exists seems crazy," she noted, marveling at the thought.

"Right? I have to tell you, these people on Terk's team have skills, serious skills. I don't even know all of what they can do myself. It's daunting to think that I would be coming in so green, but the fact that we can talk telepathically? Apparently it means that we belong with them," he shared, with a laugh.

"You mean, *you* belong with them," she clarified, with a smile. "You got a direct invitation. I didn't." She had to admit she felt a bit envious, and a hint of jealousy filled her tone. "The thought of being safe and knowing that the people around you knew what you could do and you didn't have to hide it?" she noted in wonder. "That would be amazing."

"I think that's one of the biggest things that they offer," Sanders replied. "The wonder of it all, being safe, using what you can do for good, and not having people persecuting you for what you can do? That's huge." He smiled at Ania. "You spoke to Terk already, didn't you?"

"Well, I listened. I was under the van, and suddenly he was talking to me. Who did the talking is a fine point of distinction, but one I'm sure we need to make."

"Got it," he murmured, as he checked his rearview mirror.

"What are you looking for?" she asked suddenly.

"Not looking for anything really, but I'm watching a vehicle that has been on our tail for a while, since we left the gas station."

"Oh, shit," she muttered, twisting in her seat to look behind them, her fear returning with a vengeance. "Do you think they're following us?"

"They're heading in our direction, but does that mean they're following us? I'm not exactly sure," he replied. "They're keeping their distance, and I don't even know what to think about that."

"What else will they do?" she asked. "I mean, they'll hardly run us off the road if they want us that bad."

"Maybe not," he said.

"So, are they just following us to see where we're going?"

"I don't know. I'm just keeping a wary eye on them."

"Got it. You can bet I'll keep a wary eye on them now too."

He burst out laughing. "You do that, but let's not do it in such a way that they become aware of the fact that we have noticed them."

"Right. So, secret spy mode then, right?"

"Something like that." Sanders chuckled.

"This is the work that you used to do, isn't it?"

"Before my accident, yeah," he confirmed, "but I wasn't thinking I would get back into it again because I have some injuries, and I'm not as physically fit as I've been in the past. Plus the subsequent captivity was a hard row to hoe for me in many ways, and frankly I'm still struggling to survive the effects."

"My father is an asshole," she declared.

"I can't say he's my favorite person, but I don't know whether he ordered the abuse that I suffered or not. For all I know, that was a freebie, courtesy of my individual captors. I would have preferred that they not try to break my bones and threaten me as much as they did," he muttered, "and I could have done without the torture completely." She stared, her eyes wide in horror. "Oh, shit, did you not know about that?"

She swallowed hard and shook her head. "No, I didn't," she whispered. "I'm so sorry."

He shrugged. "No, I'm sorry. I shouldn't have assumed that you knew."

"Are you okay now?"

"Getting there, but I'm dealing with residual things, like my fingers for example. They took a lot of abuse and aren't quite functioning the way I would like," he admitted, "but, hey, none of that is your fault."

"But it was my father, so doesn't that make it my fault?"

"No, not at all," he murmured. "Definitely not in my mind. Aside from the physical realities, mentally it's tough, though I suspect they were just doing their job. So I shouldn't hold it against them quite so much. A doctor I saw suggested I would do better if I could embrace forgiveness."

"*Right*." Ania rolled her eyes. "And forgiveness should be something we're all better at, I suppose, but it's easy to forgive—until you come to the big things, and then it's not that easy."

"I think most people forget that. You say you forgive them, but do you really? Some of these things are just so big and so hard to forgive that you don't even know what you're asking."

"Maybe," she murmured. "I don't know that I could ever forgive him for taking my mother and my aunt from me. Even considering just what he's done personally to me is hard to forgive, but to think that he hurt you to that extent?" She shook her head. "I'm just so embarrassed and feel like I want to punch him myself."

"If you ever get the chance, let me know because I wouldn't mind getting in a kick or two myself." She burst out laughing. Then he added in a mild and somewhat serious tone, "You know we can't though, right?"

Surprised, she looked at him. "What do you mean?"

"This is something you need to know if you'll do energy work. In this field, it's important that we keep the energy positive and loving. We have to do good in life and not revert or give in to bad vibes."

"*Hmm*. I wasn't planning on doing anything bad," she said, "but it really spoils the whole thing if we can't get a shot in to even the score every once in a while." At that, she burst out laughing, Then she saw his gaze once again go to the vehicle behind them, now gradually moving up closer. "Do you really think they're after us?"

"They're staying pretty close, and they aren't passing us and blowing by. The reality is, they could just happen to be going in the same direction, which doesn't mean a thing."

"And because it doesn't mean anything, in a way it makes it way worse," she shared. "It could be that they're after us and might do something at any moment, or they could be completely innocent."

"Exactly," Sanders agreed. "So just chill about it, and we'll continue to drive as we are. We're about an hour from the rendezvous point, and that will tell us if they're after us or not."

"Right. But we need to give a warning ahead to Riff, before we come in, right? We don't want to risk bringing them to where Riff is. I would never forgive myself if the man who rescued us was caught and captured himself."

"No, that's not in the plan," Sanders replied, with such cheerfulness that she looked at him and frowned. Then he laughed. "When I told you how these people have skills, I meant it," he murmured. "I get that you probably don't understand what that means, but I think we'll be safe."

She let out a deep breath. "I hope so because I feel like we've been on the road forever. Yet we're still not even close to being secure."

"Maybe not, but let's trust a little bit longer. Our skills and instincts haven't done us wrong yet, and I'm not prepared to even think about it at the moment. Just too much is going on, so let's keep driving. We're nearing our destination, so I'll give Riff a warning soon. With any luck, we may just capture these guys too."

At that, she beamed. "I wouldn't mind that either, and I know I'm not supposed to want to kick them, but …"

"I think a kick here and there is fine," he suggested, with a chuckle. "We're just not allowed to beat the crap out of them unnecessarily."

"It depends," she noted. "I wouldn't beat on them very much before my hands would start hurting, but I sure wouldn't mind getting one or two kicks in."

"We'll see what we can do," he said, with a smile, as he put on his blinker and headed into the town center. "But first we have to see if they even give a crap about where we are and what we do in town." And, with that, he made the first of many turns.

SANDERS WATCHED AS the other vehicle continued to follow them, turn for turn into the city.

"Not looking good," Ania noted, fidgeting beside him.

"I agree," he murmured. He picked up the phone and handed it to her. "Hit Redial, and that should get you to Riff. Update him on our location and the fact that we have a tail."

Her hands shaking nervously, she quickly snatched the phone and did as he asked. When Riff's voice filled the car, she hit Speaker. Sanders stated, "We've had a tail the whole way. First, it was on a flat stretch of highway with few crossroads, which didn't determine one way or another if they gave a crap about us. However, now they're following us as we zigzag through the city."

"Of course they are," Riff muttered, with a note of resignation in his tone. "Stick to the plan, and I'll see if I can take them out first. What we want to do is get you inside a building, without anybody knowing which building it is."

"Yeah. So have you got some tricks to handle that?" Ania asked.

"Go to this underground parking lot first," he replied, giving its address, "and we'll change vehicles there."

So, with that, and a new location punched into the GPS, Ania hung up the phone and looked at Sanders nervously.

Sanders smiled at her. "It's all right. Our guys are on it."

"While I'm glad to know they're on top of it, who would have thought there would be such a need in the world for this craziness?"

"It's not just us in need," he noted, his tone firm but quiet. "People are in trouble all over the world. One of the reasons why I would consider doing this work with Terk's team in the future is because I've felt so useless since I got hurt and left the military service. I felt as if I had no purpose anymore, but this? … This is what I did before, and I felt as if I contributed a lot to what was really good and important work," he shared, the yearning evident in his tone.

"But, once I got injured, it seemed I had become redundant, and everybody else in the world kept moving forward in life. Yet I just came to a dead stop. It was hard, even after all the healing and rehab was over. I was at loose ends when your father found me, and I don't ever want to be in that place again," he murmured.

"Understood," she agreed, with a nervous laugh. Then she pointed up ahead. "We're coming up on the parking lot that Riff wanted us to go to."

Sanders nodded. "Now pack up as much as you can that we've brought with us. Be prepared to do a quick exit.

Expect another vehicle to pull up beside us, and we'll make a quick dash."

"The food too?"

"Yes. Grab everything. We don't want to leave behind any evidence of our presence. Let's see if we can make a clean jump from one vehicle to the next."

They still had a few more minutes of driving, and, by the time he pulled into the covered parking lot, she had everything bundled up. Even now she took the napkins and the hand sanitizer she'd found in the glove compartment and wiped down all the surfaces she could reach, then had Sanders do the same on the driver's side.

He nodded approvingly.

"I have no idea if it's enough," Ania noted, "but I figured something was better than nothing."

"You're doing just fine. When that vehicle comes, it'll be quick."

Terk added in Sanders's head, *Langdon will give you further directions, as to left, right, stop, park.*

And, with that, he pulled into the underground parking lot, following Langdon's lead. Sanders drove into an empty parking spot, flanked by two huge SUVs, in a darkened area of the underground parking level.

The vehicle tailing them drove past and carried on, with the two passengers inside keeping watch as best they could.

Then the door to the SUV beside them opened, right beside Sanders. He hopped out, and, with her sliding over in the front seat, following closely behind him, they quickly made the switch into the new vehicle, lying down in the back seat.

Then Riff reversed, turned around, and left the parking lot at a sedate pace.

As Sanders looked behind them, he said, "I don't think they saw us."

Riff nodded. "No reason for them to. I stayed in the shadows. So, as long as they were finding a place to park, it's all good."

"I hope so," Ania muttered.

And, with that, Riff pulled out onto the highway, then picked up speed and headed toward their next destination.

CHAPTER 8

O NCE AGAIN, ANIA found herself in the back seat of a large vehicle, but this time it had smoked windows. She looked over at Riff on the driver's side. "These are smoked windows."

He looked at her, one eyebrow raised, and nodded slowly.

"As in, … is this a government rig?" she asked, suspicion in her tone.

He grinned. "It is, indeed. I lifted it from a parking lot."

She stared at him. "You stole a government vehicle?"

"Sure." He shrugged. "What better way to travel than under cover of a government rig? We won't go too far anyway, and they'll find it abandoned on the side of the road somewhere, when we don't need it anymore."

She sat back and laughed. "It's a way to thumb our noses at my father anyway, isn't it?"

"Absolutely. While stealing isn't necessarily something we want to do, neither do I want to draw attention to you or to us and where we're going," Riff explained. "So, this was the best of the options I had available. Besides, we're not hurting anyone, and we won't cause any damage to the vehicle. We'll just park it somewhere for them to find later."

At that, she laughed again. "I like it." She turned to look at Sanders, noting the fatigue in his face. "You should have let me drive part of the way at least. You don't look so good."

"I'm fine," he replied, "but I'll close my eyes for five and see if I can recharge a bit."

Riff snorted. "You better connect with Clary and see if she can give you a boost because, until we hit an airplane, you won't have a whole lot of options for a true rest," Riff muttered.

"*Great.* Give me a few minutes at least." With that, he still struggled to drop off to sleep. Despite exhaustion and worry, he eventually did.

Ania looked over at Riff. "Is he asleep now?"

"I think so. At least recharging, which is just as important."

"He mentioned something about your people on the team can do all kinds of stuff."

"We do," he confirmed. "A lot of our skills most of the world doesn't even know about."

"That's what Sanders told me. It's fascinating, really."

"It is. And, considering the fact that you already talked to Terk telepathically, you obviously know something about it."

"No, I don't really know much about it at all," she replied. "I've had no training. Yet I find the whole thing fascinating."

"Obviously you have skills, and, since you can certainly communicate with Sanders here, that puts you in a whole different category. With your skills, you can do something with us on a professional level as well."

"I'm not sure about that," she began. "I'm an accountant, but they probably don't need anybody for that."

Riff laughed. "You might be surprised. They're in a huge

growing stage, as they've started up a whole new company, so an accountant might not be a bad idea."

She looked at him. "Do you think so?" she asked, hating that such hope filled her tone.

"It's a pretty easy question to ask, and I don't think Terk would have a problem with your asking about it. Everybody there has at least some level of practical training in self-defense skills, weapons handling, and the like, just in case they are ever attacked. You probably need to love kids too," he added, as an afterthought.

She stared at him, her gaze wide. "You mean, children are involved in this?" she asked in horror.

He looked at her, a wry smile on his face. "It's apparently a side effect of working with the energy. Creative energy is creative energy, right?"

"When you say *side effect* ..."

"Let's just say that several members of Terk's team are female, and, last I heard, almost all of them are pregnant at the moment." Ania stared, her jaw open, and he nodded. "Believe me that you're not the first one to have that reaction, but the babies are a few months away from their due dates, and then it'll be all-out chaos at their place, and Terk needs more men—and women—to help tide them over, while everybody's busy with their new families."

"Good Lord," Ania muttered. "Here I was thinking it would be all these stiff military guys who decided to never have families, never have relationships." She shook her head. "Now you're telling me that they're procreating, even though their lives are in danger?"

"But their lives aren't in danger," Riff clarified. "Most of them have already been through so much danger that they know the value of appreciating life when it's offered. In this case, they've all been under attack, and even by their own government. So this is their attempt at rebuilding a world that they choose for themselves, which is why they have their own business now."

"I can understand that," she agreed. "I've finished my degree in accounting, and, if they can use an accountant, I'm in."

"Maybe you should say that a little louder for Terk," Riff suggested, with a chuckle. "Because Terk will work even harder to get you on board, if you can help straighten out the paperwork mess he's got going on at his place. And you're an *accountant*, not just a bookkeeper, right?"

"I'm an accountant," she stated. "Fully accredited, with all the perks that go along with it."

At that, Terk's voice popped into her head. *Are you looking for a job?*

God, yes. A job, a place to live, people who don't persecute or exploit me for being who I am.

His voice warmed, and he added, *I just might have something for you.*

She smiled. *One catch though.*

Yeah, what's that? he asked.

That lazy tone of his made her smile, as she heard it in her head. *I would like to stay close to Sanders, just in case. It's really hard to find friends in this world,* she explained, stumbling over her words. *And the other part is a little hard to ask for much more than what you're already doing, but I'm still trying to get out of a country that's trying to put me in jail for being what I am,* she added. *So, a little more help on the rescue side of life, and then, hey, I'll be more than happy to straighten out your paperwork.*

You have no idea what you're offering, he warned her,

with a laugh, *but I'll take you up on it regardless. You can always quit after you've been here for a while.*

Quitting is not part of my nature, she declared. *And, while we're at it, if you've got any way to help me develop some of these energy skills that I seem to have stumbled into, all the better. I'm all yours.*

And that, Terk replied, *is the best news I've heard yet. Done. You've got a job. We just have to get your ass back over here, you and Sanders both.*

AS THE VEHICLE jerked suddenly to the right, Sanders woke from an easy sleep. They shifted positions and he was now sitting in the front passenger seat. He looked over and quickly checked, assessing the situation to see tense faces around him. "What just happened?" he murmured, coming out of his sleep abruptly.

"Looks like we've been found again," Riff noted. "I'm not sure how, but we'll take it to mean that somebody saw us do the switch, which is very unfortunate."

"Or that tracker is at work again," Sanders muttered. He turned to look behind him to see a pasty-faced Ania staring up at him mutely. He reached out a hand, and she grasped it. "It's fine," he told her calmly. "Remember that this is what we do."

She smiled. "It might be what you *did,* but you haven't been in this field for a while."

"Still, it's not exactly something you forget," he pointed out, his tone wry. "So this isn't all that bad."

"Maybe not, but it's as bad as I ever want it to get."

"And that's a good point," he noted. "Besides, if we can

get you to England, I'm sure you'll be safe enough there."

"I should have asked Terk about that," she muttered. When Sanders frowned at her, she shrugged. "I had a conversation with Terk, and apparently they could use an accountant."

He started to chuckle, even as the vehicle swerved from one side to the other. "Trust Terk to find a job skill he can use and try to hire you for it," he muttered.

"You got a problem with that?" she asked, her gaze intent.

He beamed at her. "Nope, I'm delighted. It will definitely give us a chance to get to know each other."

"And here I thought we knew each other pretty well," she replied, with an eye roll, almost getting tossed to the side of the vehicle.

"If you guys want to keep your courtship a little quieter," Riff muttered, "I'm a little busy."

"Perfect, then you won't mind what we say," she replied.

He laughed out loud. "Quite true. I've got other things on my mind than your love life."

"No love life, that's the problem," she muttered.

At that, Sanders burst out laughing too. "I'm right here," he pointed out. "But rest assured that we can take care of that, just as soon as we get rid of these guys."

"I hope you mean that," she said, "because I really don't want to end up back in this life again."

"Not liking life on the run all the time, *huh?*" he asked, with a wry look.

"Absolutely not," she muttered. "I'm all about peace. I'll happily handle all the paperwork Terk can throw at me, before I would volunteer for another trip like this."

"Let's get you home, safe and sound," Sanders noted,

"and then we'll deal with the consequences of bucking your father."

She stopped and stared at him. "Oh, crap, I didn't even consider that. Will he make life difficult for you?"

"Oh, no doubt he'll try," Sanders acknowledged, shaking his head. "Yet that's really not part of today's discussion."

"Yet maybe it should be," she muttered, staring at him, her skin pale. "He's really not a nice man."

"Oh, I think we figured that out," Sanders agreed, chuckling. "But again, that's not your problem, not today. Let's get you away, safe and sound. Then we'll work on dealing with him on a long-term basis after this."

She sank back, grimacing. "It would be much nicer if he would just let me go."

"As your father, he clearly sees a monetary value in your skills. So do you ever really think he'll truly just let you go?"

"No, not at all. Still, I would rather he gave a crap about me," she muttered. "Yet why should I be surprised, when it's all too obvious that he killed both my mother and my aunt. I haven't even had time to cry—although I feel more of an urge to scream—because my own father is a murdering chaos agent in my life—and now yours. My father's all about what I can do for him. Power hungry is what he is, and that is all about control. No love in that."

Sanders groaned. "It's aligned with the old-fashioned dowry, or whatever the price tag may be called, in order to have those daughters bring in money and food for their family. It's an antiquated custom, borne out of a lack of money and a kingdom with serfs and the mentality that men are more elevated than women and can tell you what to do. It makes for transactional marriages instead of those based on mutual love and shared values. This is the twenty-first century, for heaven's sake."

"In many ways I have been living that life, but my mother definitely had that mentality thrust upon her. So my father is not one to give up on something like that very easily, but that doesn't mean I'll let him do this to me anymore."

"Good," Sanders agreed. "Keep up that fighting spirit. It'll help you to continue this battle, … in case things get ugly."

She paled at that and sank back against the seat.

Sanders didn't want to scare her, but it was important for Ania to understand that they weren't out of danger, and, if things got ugly, the consequences could be rough, … for both of them. Maybe for all three of them. Yet Sanders would do everything he could to avoid being a prisoner again, and neither would he let Ania back into her father's hands.

He watched as the vehicle behind them careened around the corner, almost tipping over. He smiled. "They certainly don't have the same experience, do they?"

"No, they sure don't, and that's a godsend right now," Riff muttered, as he took another hard corner. "But they also could very well have far more support than we do on the ground, and that's something we have to keep in mind."

"Meaning there could be other vehicles and more people after us?" Ania asked, clearly not happy to hear that.

"Exactly. And those other vehicles aren't necessarily a problem either, unless they're able to bring us to a complete stop," Riff pointed out. "Then that's a whole different story."

"I presume at that point in time, you'll ghost?" Sanders asked.

"Absolutely. I'll do what I can to keep you guys from

getting picked up, but, as long as one of us ghosts, a chance exists for coming back around again."

"I get it," Sanders replied. "You do what you have to do."

"And particularly coming up here," Riff noted. "If I can throw them off, I'll give you the vehicle or transfer you to another one, and you'll have to keep running, until we find another location to get you out of this country," he explained, still trying hard to shake the tail. "Or—and this might be the better solution—I can get you to a safe place, then disappear, while we figure out where to take you from here."

"Either way works for me," Sanders replied comfortably. "Just so you know, I'm not getting taken alive again. I was a prisoner once, and it's not happening again."

Riff shot him a hard look and nodded. *Understood, but remember somebody else is involved now.*

I know, Sanders agreed, *and that will make a difference, but I still won't get taken.*

"Good. Keep that thought paramount, and chances are you can get out of this. Besides, these guys have to run out of people sooner or later."

At that, Ania broke in from the back seat. "Not for a while. My father commands quite a decent-sized group of goons, and they're all pretty loyal to him because he keeps their paychecks flowing nicely. They won't walk away from this if they can get kudos for bringing us in."

"Nobody's getting kudos for bringing me in," Riff declared, with a smile. "And, with any luck, we can keep you guys out of there as well. It will be much easier to *keep* you out now than to try and *get* you out again later."

CHAPTER 9

BEFORE ANIA HAD even realized it, amid all the tosses and turns, they'd pulled into a small underground parking lot, where she had been ushered out of the rig and out of the building, then around the back to yet another building. She didn't say a word and just followed the instructions she had been given, keeping up with the men, as they raced from one building to the other. When they slipped inside a small apartment, she took a slow, deep breath, then let it out all at once. When she could breathe normally again, she asked, "Did we lose them?"

"For the moment, yes," Riff noted calmly. "Now I suggest you guys catch up on some sleep, and I'll be back." And, with that, he turned, walked out the door, and was gone.

She stared at Sanders. "How are you holding up?"

"I'm doing pretty well," he said, panting mildly.

Still, she watched in concern, as his color fluctuated, almost like a wand waving in front of her. "Actually you don't look very well at all."

He winced. "Let's just say I'm relying on other people's energy a little more than I would like to right now."

"And that is not good," she cried out in alarm. "If you go down, I won't have any way to move you."

He laughed. "Is that your way of telling me that I'm fat?"

"No, but you're huge, and fat has nothing to do with it," she stated. "I'm not very big, and I sure don't have the muscle to move you, so you need to stay mobile for my sake, if nothing else."

"Got it," he said, sending her a careless grin.

But she glared at him. "I mean it."

"I know you do," he replied, his tone softening. He walked over, wrapped her up in his arms, and just held her close.

It took her a minute, and then she finally sagged against him. "Dear God, I so want this over with."

"It may not feel like it, but we're making progress."

Her snort was loud and completely spontaneous. She lifted her head to see Sanders's big grin. "Are you trying to lie to me, or are you being serious?"

"I'm being very serious," he stated. "I try not to lie if I don't have to."

She wrapped her arms around him, hugged him gently, and sighed. "I think we should probably rest."

"Oh, I agree. You got any way to shut all this down in your head?"

She winced. "No, I don't, but, if you've got any way that might work, I'm more than happy to listen to what you have to suggest."

He smiled. "Let's check and see if we can make coffee or tea or anything else in this place. Did you bring the groceries with you?" She nodded and pointed to the bag with the remaining sandwiches. "Good, then we won't need more food tonight."

"No, I can live on sandwiches for quite a while," she shared, looking over at him. "How about you?"

"Hey, it's food. I don't really care what it is. As long as I get to eat, I'm fine. I only really need the food because of the energy."

"Which is a hell of a good reason," she noted, looking at him. "All of us need food for energy, by the way."

At that, he chuckled. "I have my laptop here and my phone, so let's check in with the rest of the team and see if anybody's got a plan to get us out of here."

While he walked over to the couch and sat down, setting up the electronics on the coffee table, she walked into the small kitchen and took a look around. She didn't know where they were, whether this was a vacant house or someone lived here. A little bit of food was in one of the cupboards, but not much, and nothing was in the fridge, so obviously nobody was living here at the moment. In a way that made her feel better. She didn't want to think that she was taking over somebody's house. Yet, if she was, she sent up a prayer, with a whisper of thanks for at least having the space available.

As she came back out, she announced, "Nothing really here, not even a coffeepot, but I found coffee, if you think it's okay to heat it in a pot on the stove."

"Absolutely, put it on," he replied.

"Will we have to erase any tracks of being here?"

He stopped and frowned at her. "That'll be much harder if we stay here for long," he admitted, "and I suggest that we might as well at least get comfortable and hope that we'll be here for only a day or two."

She winced. "I would rather hope that we can get out of here and spend the next day or two in England."

"I agree with you, or I would, except we've been tagged again. So, for right now, it's pretty hard to say."

"Sure, but won't they just go door to door around here?

It is possible, right?"

"I'm not sure if you noticed, but we got quite a bit farther away than I would have expected. Riff's very good, and he seems to have some ability to ghost people."

She walked into the living room and sat down beside him, then asked in a curious tone, "What does that mean? I heard you and Riff discussing that in the car earlier."

"I don't know exactly," Sanders admitted, with a wave of his hand. "I think Terk's people have abilities and skills that have never even occurred to us, and I know that Riff's a shadow and that he works in the shadows. He mentioned that twice, so it makes me wonder if he doesn't have a way of somehow … throwing other people off." He gave her a smirk. "That probably sounds like invisibility or cloaking or some complete garbage, so don't worry about it. I'm just rambling now, hoping and all."

"It might not be complete garbage," she noted slowly. "But it's an interesting theory, isn't it?"

"I've certainly seen situations where we could have used something like that or cloaking or whatever. So, I don't know if he did or he didn't," Sanders said cautiously. "Therefore, I can't say that Riff or anyone else did that for sure, but, if they could do it, I'm all for it and would love to have that skill too."

"Yeah, you and me both," she muttered, staring at him. "That skill alone would be a really good reason to go work for Terk. If they can do anything at all like that, I would very much like to know how."

"But it's not just about *how*," Sanders pointed out. "I think it's all about doing it, putting in the practice, putting in the time to build whatever skills are needed, in order to do these kinds of things. That's potentially what Terk's place and being a part of their team would mean. For both of us."

"Meaning that we would have to commit. It's not a simple case of *go there, be a part of it, and get to leave.* We would have to commit to it."

"Yes. I think it's very much a case of commitment, and, after what they've done for me already, I have no problem doing that," he declared. "As long as they're on the right side of the law and helping people, I'm totally okay to help in return. Not to mention that it would be really great to feel like I fit in somewhere."

Immediately she nodded. "Yes, … that. And considering that we still need their help and that we're not out of danger and that we will likely need their help on the other side of this, it's probably even a better idea."

"It's one of those cases where we're stronger together," Sanders noted calmly, "than we are apart."

"Yet, who knew that we would be weak in any case." She laughed. "But, if you say so, I will take your word for it. I'll go put on coffee, and maybe we will have better luck at thinking straight."

"Yes, coffee," he muttered. "Although I did get some sleep, I didn't get a lot."

She nodded. "You should crash." He hesitated, but she shook her head. "No. It's obvious that you need to get some more sleep. I will too, so we'll do it in relays."

He smiled at her. "We call them *watches.* I'll take four hours, and then you take four hours," he suggested simply. "But, in any normal circumstance, I wouldn't let you take any."

"Yeah, well, that's great," she muttered in exasperation, "but absolutely nothing is normal about this. Neither is anything normal about the fact that your energy is at the end of its thread. You look as if you may collapse at any time. So you need to do something to look after yourself. You can't always depend on these other people to keep you alive."

"I wasn't planning on it," he noted, still smiling. "So go put on the coffee, and I'll do what I can to get a little rest, just as soon as I connect with everybody and fill them in."

With that, she headed into the kitchen and rummaged around, starting the coffee, not sure exactly how old it was. When she had a pot of water on to heat up, the grounds already added, she stepped into the living room to check on him, finding him stretched out on the couch.

Just as she went to tiptoe past him, he reached out a hand and said, "Wake me up in two hours."

"No, I'll wake you up in four." He opened his eyes and glared at her. She shrugged. "If you couldn't even stay awake long enough to have some of the coffee I just made, no way I'll let you sleep for only two hours. Then, in four hours, you can make more coffee."

His lips twitched, but his gaze collapsed inward, as he dropped into a deep, exhausted sleep.

She sat here on the couch, watching him, more worried than she could put into words. Seeing him go out that fast was scary. Sanders didn't have the resources to hold himself for long. Knowing that he was relying on other people for that energy, that strength was incredibly disconcerting to Ania. It also made her feel alone here in many ways, a situation that she'd never experienced before. It was lonely, and it was stressful.

As she returned to the kitchen, she strained the coffee and now sat on the chair, sipping a hot cup of joe. She didn't dare go to sleep, so she opened her loaner phone and checked for messages, even while knowing that she didn't dare contact anybody. But when a text message came through from Vanessa, she opened it and read it to see a question.

How are you?

Ania hesitated for a moment because it was possible her friend Vanessa hadn't sent this herself, or she may be under duress. Did Ania dare reply, or would it be traceable? The possibility glared at her.

Immediately Terk slammed into her head. *Don't answer.*

She almost bolted upright, it was such a shock. She responded and asked, *Can you turn down the volume a little?*

As long as you listen, yes, Terk declared in a harsh tone. *Don't you dare give anyone any indication of where you are. Absolutely no electronic tracking allowed.*

Oh, I get it. I just don't know how they found us here at all.

It wouldn't take too much, he muttered. *People who have skills and abilities, hackers even, but especially if they have an energy-working tracker on their side,* he explained, with a note of wariness in his tone. *So you're still not out of danger.*

At that, she winced. *Right, the tracker finding me at the hotel,* she whispered. *He needs to not come for at least four hours because Sanders is out cold. I hate to say it, but he's not looking very well.*

He's been burning up too much energy. He's not fully healed. He's had a lot of muscle-wasting over the last six months in captivity, and his energy is just not there yet. So, while his body is trying to heal, he's burning through his own energy, therefore, other people are required to keep him functioning. That sleep is very important. He should be good for a few hours and after that on his own, but then we'll have to help again.

It just boggled the mind to even think that such a thing was possible, but Ania's first thought instinctively was, *Can I help him too?*

You can, but not right now. He's in a rejuvenating sleep. Let him rest for now. Let him sleep. The healers are filling his system with more energy, trying to heal some of the muscle damage that he had. He really needed a few months to recover and to get back in the gym to build up some of that muscle he lost, before he came after you. However, once he realized he was up and semi-functioning, he wouldn't take no for an answer. It was much more efficient to send Riff to help rescue you and to let Sanders go on this op, than it was to argue with him and try to keep him down at our castle, where he would feel imprisoned all over again.

She understood that, but one of Terk's words caught her attention. *You guys live in a castle?* she asked cautiously.

He snorted. *Yeah, no kidding,* he said, with a laugh. *Not exactly the best decision I've ever made, but I think everybody else in the team might disagree.*

If it's got a moat and a swimming pool and massive gardens, she replied, *I'm not against it.*

It's got all of that and more, or at least in the future planning stages, he replied. *We just have to get you here. Our original escape plans have gone awry, but we're on to plan B right now. Riff should be back to your place within about four hours.*

Is it okay that I made coffee? she asked.

It is, he replied. *If you get a warning with some time to clean up after you, that's good too. But, if you don't get a warning, we'll send in a cleaning crew afterward anyway.*

Do you really think somebody will come here and check?

Nope, it's a safe house. I got access to it from a friend of mine. We just prefer to keep things clean. Imagine coming back because you need a safe house and finding moldy coffee and all that stuff lying around.

Oh, gross, she said instantly.

He laughed. *Exactly. So, we'll just get somebody in to clean it up, if you can't.*

I was hoping Sanders could get some coffee. I'll have a couple cups, but, once he's awake again, I think he'll need that and the rest of the sandwiches.

If you can sleep, sleep, Terk noted. *You're not exactly all that solid yourself.*

She frowned. *I'm fine. Besides, one of us needs to keep watch.*

Actually, Terk offered, his tone calm, *I can keep watch on both of you. So, if you've had your coffee, just curl up beside him and let yourself sleep.*

She instinctively shook her head. *That would be foolish,* she murmured. *Somebody needs to stand watch over him.*

Two healers are standing watch over him right now, he muttered. *And I'm not far behind. So you take care of yourself, so that you're ready to run if we need you to.*

She sighed. *I will, but I really wanted the coffee, even if I had to heat it on the stovetop in a pan and then filter out the grounds.*

You might want to consider a microwave cup of instant coffee next time, he suggested, with a note of humor in his tone.

Great, she muttered. *But, hey, it's coffee, and it's warm. I'll finish this cup, then see how I feel about taking a nap.*

You can do that, but, if I find your energy is dropping, I won't be happy.

Ania frowned.

And, yes, I can tell. And, yes, it's important that you run when you need to, he murmured. *So, I know I'm being a bit of a hard-ass about it, but you would do well to listen.* She didn't like hearing that, and he waited for her to argue.

It's not as if I can say anything about it, she muttered. *You've got the upper hand.*

No. I have the experience. I don't care about the upper hand, he corrected instantly. *I'm trying to keep my people safe. And, if you'll be one of my people, you need to follow orders too.*

Fine. As long as you won't imprison us.

That would be the last thing I would ever do, he said, his tone gentle. *This is all about keeping Sanders safe too. We went to a lot of effort to rescue him and a lot of work to heal him, as much as he would let us. So, when he wakes up, he still won't be fully functioning, and I need you there to help him.*

Immediately she felt like a heel. *I'm sorry. I guess I'm punchier than I thought.*

It goes along with being exhausted, he said, the humor back in his tone. *But, when you're in on a deal like this, there can't be any arguments. We all work together.*

I'm not trying to argue, she whispered. *I just want to go home.* Then she realized what she'd said. *Correction, I no longer have a home. So let me just say that I want this all to stop. I just want to be safe.*

And you're close, Terk noted. *You're very close to that, so let's not do anything to blow it up now.* And, with that, he was gone.

She got up, looked down at the coffee that she really didn't want anymore, but, unable to waste it, she tossed back the rest of it and walked the cup back into the kitchen. She looked at the leftover coffee in the saucepan she'd made, a small one at that, but it even seemed wrong to leave it there. Yet she could microwave the leftovers in the morning, if need be.

She headed back to the small loveseat beside the couch,

curled up in a corner, and crashed. She had no doubt that, whatever Terk's abilities, when he stated that she needed to rest, he meant it. Whether she liked it or not, he was also right, and that was a little hard to get used to. She wasn't used to having people able to read her and to say *It's time for you to go down for a nap.*

Matter of fact, her life had seemed awfully sheltered up until her mother's death. After that, everything had gone to hell. And, on that last thought, she closed her eyes and slept.

SANDERS WOKE SUDDENLY, not with any sense of alarm that something was wrong, just a full-on awareness. He slowly sat up, then looked over to see Ania curled up on the loveseat, her breath soft and peaceful as she slept deeply. He was surprised that she had gone down, as she had been so insistent on standing watch. Yet it was a good thing she had because, once they had to get moving, he needed her awake and alert, mentally and physically. In his current condition, it would be hard for him to carry her, but he would if he needed to. That was a given, but he didn't know how long he could keep it up, so best that it not be needed.

Terk's voice filled his head. *She was run down too, so I had her crash. She didn't want to. She was insistent on standing guard over you.*

Yeah, I think she feels responsible in many ways because I came back to get her.

Of course, Terk agreed, a smile in his tone. *It's obvious that she cares about you.*

We've been through a lot together, Sanders said, his tone gentle. *And I know that it's not over yet, but I sure don't want anything to happen to her.*

We're doing our best to ensure it doesn't, and remember that it's not just you. Other people are involved here. We'll do our best to get you both out.

I know. I know, and I'm sorry. You're right. I just thought maybe I would be stronger.

What you took for your strength was other people's healing ability at work in you, Terk explained. *Frankly the energy required to keep you here was more than what we're spending now, so it's been worth it. In the end, sending you after her was the less expensive option, energy-wise. And, hey, if she's an accountant, I can really use her here,* he added, with a note of humor.

She also has some abilities that may be of benefit to you as well.

Maybe. Currently she's untrained, so pretty scattered, and doesn't understand what she can do.

She's spent more of her lifetime hiding her gifts than opening up and trying to do anything with them, Sanders explained. *I don't blame her for that.*

Neither do I, Terk agreed. *It just makes me think even more about opening a training center here because, as we're discovering, an awful lot of people out there have skills, but not everybody has them defined or even understands what they can do. Like so many things in life, opportunities pass us by because we didn't take the time to develop them.*

Sanders nodded. *Yet it's really amazing she's done what she has. When you think about it, she hasn't had any training or any opportunity to do something like this, and still her gifts are showing up. What she really needs is just a chance to settle down, to relax, maybe to play with this a little. I think, when she has the time and place to do that, then she'll see that she's got more potential than she realizes.*

She is doing very well, Terk noted, *and the fact that she can communicate telepathically as easily as she can means an awful lot is there for us to work with. Yet she needs to come on her own because it has to be what she wants, not because it's what she feels she has to do.*

Do you think that's what she's thinking? Sanders asked. *I hope it's not because of me.*

I'm sure it is *because of you,* Terk stated, with a laugh. *She cares for you, and she needs a new life. Just ensure that the relationship you develop comes from mutual understanding and not just gratitude.*

Yeah, when you think about it, we're two prisoners thrown adrift, Sanders admitted. *In many ways we have an awful lot in common.*

You absolutely do, and that's a good thing in many ways, Terk noted, his tone calm. *I just want you both to experience some freedom and ensure that whatever relationship you end up with comes together for the right reasons.*

And, with that, he rang off.

CHAPTER 10

ANIA WOKE WITH a start to a hand, gentle, yet firm, pressing against her shoulder. She looked up to see Sanders sitting on the edge of the loveseat, a finger to his lips.

She nodded slowly. "Somebody's here?" she asked in a low voice.

He shook his head, his tone equally low and whispered back, "People are outside, looking around, searching the place. I just didn't want them to hear us, to see us, or to attract any energy to find us, you know?"

She slowly let out her breath. "I have to get used to the idea that just even thinking about such a thing can attract unwanted attention," she murmured.

"Sorry to wake you, but you should be up and ready to go, if we need to bolt." She winced at that but got up and stretched. He handed her a cup of coffee, which she accepted gratefully. "It would be good to wait a bit to use the bathroom, if you can."

"Right. No toilet flushing to give us away. Any food left?" she asked softly.

"Still one sandwich left over from last night. Riff was here, and he's gone again."

"Of course he is." She shook her head. "I don't suppose he brought us another vehicle or has a plan or anything like that, does he?"

He gave her a fat grin. "A bit of both."

"That's good, but was the interest outside a part of the plan?"

"Nope. We're not even sure it had anything to do with us, but we're going on the assumption that any interest in this direction is bad news. Definitely bad news."

"I won't argue with that," she murmured. "Just tell me when we're ready to bolt."

"Hopefully we won't have to, and we can stay here for a couple days."

"Actually," she replied, giving him an intent look, "I would much prefer to bolt and to get the hell out of here than to deal with spending a couple more days waiting for somebody to find us. If we can get *gone*, that would be the best. I just want to get that flight to England."

He nodded. "I hear you there, but we can't do it without making sure we're safe first."

She knew he was right and wouldn't argue with that. She just wanted that safety factor balanced with the get-out-of-jail-free-card factor. Not that he would understand that, but she was feeling the pressure in a way she hadn't really expected.

He squeezed her hand gently. "Just remember that everybody's on this, and they all have a vested interest in getting us out of here. They're on it."

She almost cracked a smile of that. "Do we know for sure that it's a good idea to go to them?" she asked suddenly. "I mean, is there any reason to worry about joining this group? I've not had any experience with them."

"I haven't had that much myself," Sanders conceded, his tone calm and yet reassuring. "But remember that we can tell who these people are just from reading them."

"I thought I could," she muttered, "but the drugs are still affecting my results."

"They will for a while. Still, you trust Riff, don't you?"

"Unfortunately, yes, I do," she said, with a soft laugh. "He's not the easiest person to talk to, but I don't doubt that what he says is what he means, but so many…" She hesitated. "It's like so many blank spots are in his world that, although I trust him, I don't know how far I trust him."

"Now that's a very interesting assessment," Sanders noted, "on the blank spots."

"I don't know whether it's true or not. It's just that I, … since I can't see all of him, I don't know what part of him I can trust. I'm sorry. … I trust what I can see, I just don't know about the other parts."

"Good enough," Sanders said. "I don't think any of us can trust everyone 100 percent anyway, not until we know them better at least, and we don't know any of these people all that well. Let's not make assumptions. But what we do know is that we've had, and continue to have, an awful lot of people behind us, and they are here to help us."

"I guess that's what I'm still questioning," she murmured. "I want to trust everybody, yet it seems foolhardy at this point in time."

At that, his phone vibrated. He looked around the apartment. "This could be the call to get out of here." He answered it, his tone calm, steadfast. "Hi, Terk. … Yes, I am aware that people are interested in this area. We've got the curtains closed, lights off, and are keeping our energy as calm and as low as we can, while we wait for Riff to get back. He was here earlier but headed out to do some recon."

Ania listened to the conversation a little bit more, and,

when Sanders hung up, he turned and shared, "Riff has checked in with Terk, and it appears that the interest was more in our direction. He thinks they're using a human tracker, who may be having problems finding you, probably because of the drugs in your system, which is also why you're having trouble reading other people."

She blinked several times and then nodded. "I guess that's the only good thing to come from being drugged, at least as far as I can see."

He chuckled. "But it's great that they're struggling to find us. That's a good thing for us."

"Absolutely," she murmured. "Though it's not that big of a help if it's preventing us from getting out of here safely."

"We'll go, but not until we're sure it's safe to leave the building."

She winced and nodded. "So, we're sitting ducks until then."

"Exactly. So, let's ensure everything's packed up and cleaned up, even if we have to unpack later. But let's set ourselves up to leave it in the best shape that we can."

Following his lead, she got up and washed the few dishes they'd used, drying them and putting them back in the cupboards. Just as she was done, she sat down on the couch next to him and asked, "Next?"

His smile was rueful. "Same as last time, we'll just sit and wait."

She winced. "Not exactly my favorite activity."

"Mine either," he murmured. "But neither is being hunted."

As conversation stoppers went, that was a good one. She sank back onto the couch, then scrubbed her face. "You don't realize what a toll this takes on you when you're in the middle of it. Then, all of a sudden, you get a couple minutes to breathe, and you can see just how devastating this has been to your system." She held up her hand, and it trembled ever-so-slightly.

He pulled her into his arms and just rocked with her gently.

"I didn't show you that to make you feel sorry for me. That is definitely not what I was trying to do. It's just long-term stress."

"I get that," he commented, with a smile. "But you also need to know that we won't let them get you again."

"Maybe not, but you were also captured, so you should be just as freaked out."

He chuckled at that. "I can't say that I'm *just* as freaked out, but I definitely don't want to be. That is not how I want to end up again. So, I put my trust in Terk and his team. I honestly believe in what they're doing and how they're doing it. That alone makes it a little bit easier, knowing we have such a powerful group helping us."

"You have that firsthand experience," she noted calmly. "I don't."

"I get that too. But remember that a lot of effort was made to get you out of that scenario you were in. The fact that you escaped by yourself is huge and should give you a little sense of what you can do on your own, if you have to. Obviously we don't want that for you, but you've come a long way, and that's just as important. Now it's a matter of fine-tuning the possibilities, making sure that we don't have to deal with this ever again."

"How does that happen?" she murmured. "I mean, short of threatening my father, how do we let him know that he'll never get away with this again?" When he hesitated, she nodded. "See? You don't have any answers either."

"I might not have answers," he began, "but I also have no problem doing whatever I need to do in order to get them." When she looked at him quizzically, he sighed. "If threatening your father is what we need to do in order to ensure he doesn't come after you again, I'm all for it. You may have a problem with it, but I do not."

"I don't have a problem with it either," she declared. "If my mother were still alive, I would be rethinking all of this, but I also wouldn't be in this position. I don't know what he knows about me, and I don't really want to have that conversation with him because I'm quite liable to let something loose in the entire process."

He chuckled. "It could also be that he has other gifted people on salary, or found other gifted people, and they told him. It may not have had anything to do with your mother's death, aside from maybe relaxing the morality or the bonds holding him back from testing you. Once you decided that you were fighting and were leaving, then he was in the position of having to do something about it."

"It's almost as if you sympathize with him," she suggested, staring at him suddenly.

His eyebrows shot up. "Absolutely not. I have no sympathy for anybody who kidnaps and detains people against their will, much less kills those who won't conform. Remember that I'm just as much of a victim of your father as you are."

Her shoulders sagged. "God, this is making me crazy. It's also driving me nuts that I can't tell friend from foe right now. That was something I could always count on, and I hadn't realized how much I depended on it. It seems that everything is slipping."

"Why wouldn't you depend on it?" he asked. "It's held you in good stead, and, for the most part, you've been very blessed to have people you could read. But people like Riff? They've spent a lifetime stopping others from reading them. They lock down parts of themselves, and they're very private and don't appreciate it if anybody steps inside their boundaries."

"I've probably already done that," she admitted. "Not intentionally, of course, just not realizing he had put up walls and boundaries to stop me. I was just trying to figure out what I was getting from him, and there were all these walls."

"He would have let you know, just as he lets everybody else know, exactly how far you're allowed into his world. When he doesn't want you in there, believe me that you won't be in there anymore."

She burst out laughing. "I'm already at that point, since he butted me out a while ago."

Sanders grinned. "Me too. And that's okay. It's all part and parcel of learning to work with people who have abilities. … If we don't have any boundaries set, can you imagine what our own personal lives would be like?" he asked, waggling his eyebrows at her. "Do you really want them knowing everything about our world?"

She flushed, then shook her head. "God, no, good point. I hadn't really considered it from a boundary perspective, but you're right. It's not what any of us want to have or to see from others."

"It's an easy line to cross. It's just one of those things to be aware of and to spend a little more time making sure we don't upset people over it."

She sighed at that. "I think we'll make a lot of mistakes."

"I don't think they'll hold any mistakes against us

though," he suggested. "This isn't like some testing."

"Are you sure?" She sent him a sideways glance.

Just then, a knock came on the door. She bolted to her feet, feeling the fear, then her feet slid out from under her, as fear sent her crashing back down onto the couch, with a fist shoved into her mouth. He gave her a hard look, his hand squeezing hers, and shook his head. When nobody answered the door, another hard knock came. When nothing happened, she started to relax, until she heard somebody working at the lock.

She looked over at Sanders and saw his jaw firm up, as he slowly stood. With a finger to his lips, he leaned over and whispered, "Go into the bedroom. This guy will come in, even though he's not welcome, and I'll take care of him."

And, with that, he nudged her toward the bedroom.

WITH HIS EAR up against the nearby wall, Sanders listened to confirm whether just one or two people were trying to work their way inside. He heard a conversation farther down the hallway, and the work on the lock stopped for a moment. Then it quickly resumed, and faster, as if somebody was out of time and panicking. He was definitely out of time because, as soon as this guy opened the door, he would get a fist in the jaw from Sanders.

He cast a glance back to ensure Ania had listened and was out of sight and out of the firing line, in case this guy had a weapon. Sanders knew it wasn't Riff because he would have gotten in much faster. So, this was somebody else, unfortunately with shitty timing because Sanders didn't have a way to get Ania out of here just yet. Just then he heard a man calling out.

"Hey, what are you doing? That's my apartment."

The tone was hard, yet the man's voice was completely recognizable, as he shouted down the hallway.

A momentary stillness came from the person working on the lock, then another voice close by said, "This isn't your apartment. It's ours."

"Like hell," Riff declared, his tone furious, as he raced toward them. "You get the hell away from my place, or I'm calling the cops."

Other apartment doors started to open, but Sanders didn't hear anybody else joining the conversation. Those doors closed as quickly as they opened, as if people recognized trouble when they saw it. Most people were quick to bounce right back out of any confrontation, not having anything to do with it. They were right in most cases, and these weren't the guys who civilians wanted to argue with either. However, Sanders and Riff had no choice.

Riff seemed to be right there, arguing with one of the guys, so Sanders quickly pulled open the door, grabbed the nearest guy, and dragged him into the apartment, giving him a solid right hook and dropping him to the floor.

When the door opened a second time, Riff brought in the second man and nodded approvingly. "That's a good trick. I'm getting damn tired of running," he muttered.

Sanders agreed with a nod. "I figured we better get some answers and fast."

Ania was suddenly at his side. She threw her arms around his neck, hugged him close, and then turned to face Riff. "What's going on out here?" she asked, trembling, almost in tears. She was beyond pale.

He just smiled. "We caught these two trying to break

into the apartment. Smart move on Sanders's part to bring them inside. Now they are captives for a change."

She looked down at the men, with evident loathing. "These men work for my father," she stated. "Why would we want anything to do with them?"

"What we want is answers," Sanders replied. "We can't keep running."

She shuddered but nodded. "Or we could just lock them up, still unconscious, and leave."

"We could, but how long would it be before they or some of the others were right on our tails again?"

Her shoulders slumped, and she went and sat down on the couch. "What do you expect them to tell you?" she asked, the curiosity in her tone finally overriding the fear of facing these men. "I mean, once they realize there are three of us and that Sanders is involved again, it won't go well for you, if they capture you again."

"It won't sit right with me anyway," Sanders replied, a sense of reassurance filling his tone. "Anybody who's escaped already won't have an easy time if recaptured. That includes you and me. They won't hold back, no matter what, now."

She didn't say anything but glared at the two goons, both still unconscious. "What could they possibly tell us?" She looked over at Riff. "That we don't already know?"

"Maybe that's what we need to find out," he suggested. "The real issue here is, how do we stop your father from coming after you and not giving a damn? They already know that Sanders has some abilities, and the fact that we've come and rescued you will likely mean—at least in your father's mind—that you have something worth being rescued for."

She glared. "My father doesn't think I have any value at all. He's just worried I've got some monetary value or status that he's afraid he'll miss out on. So I really don't think your technique will work."

"We'll find out soon enough then, won't we?" Riff noted, with a cheerfulness that Sanders didn't feel. Riff looked back at Ania. "You might want to go into your room. It could get ugly."

She shrugged. "I'm not worried about it getting ugly. I'm worried about them coming after us in retaliation for this. If we could just get away, I don't think they would care."

"Do you want to look over your shoulder for the rest of your life?" Sanders asked. "I sure don't."

She frowned. "But this won't help."

Riff turned and smacked the guy nearest him, bringing him around quickly, now screaming in Russian. Riff dropped a hand to his throat and squeezed tightly. The gurgling noises coming out of his mouth were enough to make even a hardened specialist in this field wince.

Sanders looked over at Ania. "You probably should go into another room."

She shook her head. "No, we've started this now. I may be a mess, but I'm not walking away."

Sanders cast a glance at Riff, who just shrugged and replied, "That's fine. It's always better to know what the hell's going on than to hide, which hasn't worked very well so far." He released his grip on his captive's throat.

The man switched to English. "We will kill you for this," he warned, his tone calm, almost too calm.

Riff smiled. "You're assuming you'll live long enough," he replied.

The other man glared at him. "My boss will not take kindly to having me killed. I am far too important to him."

At that, Ania laughed. "Not even *you* are that stupid," she muttered. "You know perfectly well that my father will just hire somebody else, anybody else. You're a commodity to him."

He turned and glared at her. "You are a bad daughter."

She started to laugh. "Oh my, of all the things I was expecting to be accused of, that was not one of them." She shook her head, but then she got up and walked closer and kicked him hard. "*You* are a bad man. You kidnapped me, held me captive, helped my father to keep me drugged, and for what?" she asked, spitting the words in his face. "I didn't do anything to hurt you or him."

"You are his," he stated calmly. "You're young, and you're nothing but a woman."

"Wow, there we go again," she muttered, slowly rotating her neck. "Sometimes I just hate everything my father stands for."

His glare deepened. "Your father is a good man."

"No, not even in my wildest dreams, would I even begin to believe that crap," she muttered. She looked over at Sanders and Riff. "I suggest you get whatever information you want, and then let's get out of here."

"I have no information," the one conscious man stated, with a shrug. "We're here to do a job. We don't go home without the job done. That is all to know."

"Ah, now that sounds more like my father."

He nodded. "It's expected. He doesn't suffer fools gladly."

"He doesn't suffer fools at all. He's got one goal and one goal only, and that's to make a name for himself," she muttered. "I don't know how he thinks having me around will raise his status." She stared at the goon, and then, as if something snapped, she glared at him. "Why does he want me?"

He looked at her in confusion. "You're his daughter," he said, as if no further explanation were required.

"Yet he hasn't given a crap about me in years. Why now?"

But obviously from the confusion on his face, he didn't understand the question. Or he understood the question, but he didn't understand the nuance behind it. He shrugged and repeated, "You're his daughter. It's his right."

"No, it's *not* his right," she snapped. "I'm an adult. I can do what I want."

He sneered. "If that were the case, your father wouldn't be doing this, would he?"

With that, she got up and, without a word, turned and walked out of the living room, heading back to the bedroom.

Sanders was glad for that, and he looked over at Riff, one eyebrow raised.

Riff nodded and reached down and squeezed the guy's neck again. After he choked him for several minutes, Riff released him and said, "Now we want to know the truth. Why is he doing this? What does he want Ania for? How do we stop him?"

"No stopping him," he gasped. "What he wants, he gets. He's a very important man. He can order whatever he wants, and, if that means killing her, then that means killing her. As I said, she's a bad daughter."

"I don't believe that." Sanders glared at him. "He's ig-nored her all this time. What has changed?"

"Now he has a purpose for her, so, of course, he wants her," he replied, with a shrug. His gaze narrowed. "He wants you too. You escaped. That is not something he'll forget."

"Of course not. It's not about having me or wanting me for any particular reason. It's about revenge for beating him at his own game."

At that, the other man stiffened and declared, "You did not beat him."

"Really? So, he just let me go, did he?"

He nodded and smiled. "If you got free, he let you go."

"*Right.*" The complete blind faith in this man was enough to make Sanders want to kick him too, but he'd seen it time and time again. When it came to powerful men, they somehow managed to engender loyalty, even in spite of the obvious lies being fed to them. "You really have no idea what he was doing then, do you?"

"No, and it doesn't matter. My boss says to do something, I do it. That's what loyalty is all about." He glared at him. "You? … You know nothing of that."

"*Of course not,*" Sanders noted, with a mocking smile. "I was just a prisoner, after all. It's not as if I had any rights."

"No, and you won't again," he declared. "It will be far worse for you this time."

"If I just kill you now, it won't make a difference, will it?" Sanders asked, with a casual tone. "And since that's what you were planning on doing to me, why would I ever let you go?"

"It matters not if you let me go free," he replied, his tone stiff, but his gaze flashed wildly about. "Killing me won't stop them."

"*Them?*" Riff pounced. "Who is them?"

The goon glared and didn't say anything, until Riff squeezed his neck once more. Upon Riff's release, the goon took a breath, then muttered, "Wait, wait, wait. He has other men, lots of other men. Even if I fail, they won't."

"Why is that?" Riff asked curiously. "What? Do they have some *special* skills that will find me somehow?" he asked, deliberately using a mocking tone.

That seemed to make the goon even angrier, and he nodded. "We have *much* better skills. We have people."

"You mean *one* particular person?" Riff asked, and that garnered a response.

The goon shrugged and nodded. "But he's good, very good."

"And yet he gives you the wrong information half of the time, so how good can he be?"

He didn't like hearing that and snapped his mouth shut and just glared.

Sanders looked over at Riff and said, "Knock him out."

Riff started to squeeze his neck again, just enough to have him go unconscious.

Sanders checked the goon's pockets, grabbing his cell phone.

The other goon finally jerked awake, backtalking again. "I will kill you for that." Looking over at Riff, he added, "I will kill you."

Such a promise filled his words that Riff just smiled. "You're welcome to try but not until I'm done with you. Then you can have your chance."

His gaze narrowed again, and he went to say something, except his phone rang just then.

Sanders looked over at Riff with a question in his eye. Sanders just shrugged. "Your guess is as good as mine on this one."

Riff sat on this goon, one hand to his mouth, while his other hand grabbed the goon's phone. He answered it with a gruff voice.

A male spat out Russian, obviously irate and pissed off at his goons having either slowed something up or not having completed something on time. Riff just looked at his prisoners on the floor, one eyebrow raised, then deliberately hung up.

At that, the goon's features paled to pasty white, and he looked up at him.

"See? I don't care to talk to your friends," Riff stated, "and I really couldn't care less who they are. And, if they come here, all the better."

The goon shook his head wildly. "But they will kill me," he muttered. "You don't understand. They will kill me."

Riff just laughed, turning to Sanders.

"Actually I understand," Sanders replied. "So sorry about that. Yet you were quite happy to kill me and Ania, so what do I care if they kill you?" he asked, with real curiosity. "Don't you realize that her father killed her mother and her aunt? So why wouldn't he kill you too, if you are not doing as Ania's father says?"

That was something the goon didn't like to hear. He just clammed up and didn't say anything more.

Both goons were now tied up, while Sanders searched one and went through his wallet, with Riff searching the other for his info.

Sanders found some ID, some documentation, but not a whole lot. Also a little bit of money, but again, not very much. "He doesn't pay you very well, does he?" Sanders noted, shaking his head at the two goons.

"It is enough. It's an honor to work for him."

The stiff pride made Sanders shake his head again. "Such freaking idiots," he muttered.

"You don't understand anything," the goon snapped.

"You are not loyal."

"Oh, I'm loyal. I'm loyal to the people who count. I'm definitely not loyal to assholes who kidnap and torture and drug young women," he shared, giving this goon a hard gaze. "Whenever you think that that's an okay deal, boy, have you got it wrong."

"It's his daughter."

"And that makes a father's abuse and control all okay? Just because it's his daughter means she doesn't have any right to live her own life?"

"She has no rights," he cried out. "None of them do."

"Right, of course. We are in Russia after all," he stated, with an eye roll.

The other man obviously didn't understand what the problem was, and that was something Sanders would have to reconcile later. He didn't have time for that now. The fact of the matter was, Ania was here and was still in trouble.

When the goon's phone rang again, it was in Riff's hand. He answered it calmly, but, instead of somebody yelling and screaming at the other end, a cold voice said, "Put my man on."

"Why should I?" he asked.

"Do it."

Riff laughed. "I don't take orders from you. And we're not done causing pain in your world yet either."

"I will have you killed for this," he snapped, his voice firm with conviction and deadly with promise. "Nobody crosses me like this."

"When we take you to court for having kidnapped and drugged your daughter, and for kidnapping a British citizen and holding him prisoner for six months against his will, I wonder just what will happen to you."

"It wasn't against his will," he declared, with a laugh. "Is that what he told you? We were simply working on testing some special skills he has. Obviously he went a little crazy, but, if I'd realized he was as unstable as he was, I wouldn't have gone there in the first place."

"Nice try," Riff replied. "Don't worry. I have them here, safe and sound."

An ugly silence came on the other end of the phone. "I want my daughter back." His tone was harsh.

"Not happening, so I don't really see the point of continuing this conversation, particularly since you have nothing that I want."

"I want my daughter," he repeated. "I can go to the government and get help against British citizens who kidnapped my daughter."

"I wonder if she'll have a different story to tell," Riff said, with a laugh, "considering that we've already got her side of the story. The fact that she had to run away and to live on the streets in order to evade you, … that is just sad. What kind of a father are you that you would hurt her so much?"

"My daughter has mental problems," he stated. "She's on medication and needs another dose. Obviously we have to adjust it in order to better suit her condition."

"Yeah, so you can keep her compliant, unthinking, and there for you to abuse however you want?"

An ugly silence ensued, and then her father snapped, "That is disgusting. I would never abuse my daughter."

"Maybe not sexually," Riff clarified. "But abuse her you did, and just because we're not right in front of you at present doesn't mean that we don't have the ability to ensure you pay for this."

"This is foolish. Let me talk to my daughter."

"No, not happening," Riff declined cheerfully.

"Then I don't know that you have her, do I?"

"Doesn't matter if you know or not. We've got your two men, and we have your daughter. Believe it or not, I really don't give a crap." And, with that, Riff quickly hung up, then looked over at Sanders. "I don't think we'll get much information from these guys."

"No, I don't think so either because I don't think they know. Like any dictator, he keeps everything close, just hoping that eventually he will find a way to break them."

"He doesn't have to say anything to us," snapped the one goon, who still was conscious. "He is a very important man. He can do what he wants."

Sanders snorted. "That's the thing about the democratic society of the Western world. Nobody gets to do anything that they want. There is such a thing as making sure people's rights aren't violated."

He laughed. "In Russia, your right is only as big as the rights that you're entitled to keep. She is a woman, and, when her father wants her to do something, … it's the law."

"Right, so we're back to that power and control." Turning to Riff, Sanders said, "They don't know much, and they won't share what they do know, so why should we even bother keeping them alive? It would be much more convenient if they were just gone."

Riff nodded. "Good point, then at least we won't have to worry about these two coming after us."

"There will be others," stated the goon.

"Maybe, but you won't be worrying about it." And, with that, Riff gave him a hard chop to the neck, and he went out cold. He heard a noise behind him and turned to see Ania standing there, looking horrified.

She dashed forward. "Did you kill him?"

"No, I didn't kill him. I didn't need to. Men like these are just followers. They aren't important. They don't have much information. Seems your father isn't so much determined to keep you as much as he's determined to not lose you."

She blinked at that, and then nodded slowly. "Yes. The minute you cross him, and, particularly if you win, he has only revenge on his mind. He doesn't forgive easily," she murmured.

"He won't forgive you for leaving, so maybe you should remember that too," Riff pointed out.

"I know, but what am I supposed to do?" she asked bitterly. "Stay there as a perfect victim for the rest of my life? He would make my life miserable, … if he even lets me live at all."

"If you didn't perform the way he wanted you to, he probably wouldn't let you live."

"Exactly," she agreed, rubbing her arms. "We're all packed up. Can we leave now?"

"I think we should," Riff noted. "I want to hide these two in a couple different places, where they can't be easily found. That'll give us a good head start at least." And he carried the first man outside.

CHAPTER 11

SANDERS AND ANIA were led by Riff from the apartment into the basement of the building and now out onto the parking level, but she felt the creepiness all around her. "You know that he's watching us, right?"

"Your father's other goons are trying to, and your human tracker is trying as well. I'm sending a confusing signal in order to stop the tracker," Riff shared, "but I'm not sure it's working."

She watched, as Riff carefully slipped into an unlocked vehicle, hot-wired the car in front of her, and then opened the doors for them to get in.

Inside, she sat down and whispered, "I had no idea it was so easy to steal a vehicle."

"I think that's the second time you've mentioned something along those lines." Riff laughed. "Would you rather that we ask permission and let everybody know where we are?"

"No, because they'll already be out there waiting for us," she muttered.

It was a daunting thing to realize just how far her father had been willing to go, in order to keep her in his life. Yet she knew it wasn't out of love. The emotional aspect didn't even enter the equation. This was all about his ego now. As they slowly drove up and out of the underground parking lot, she took a deep breath and sank into the back seat, trying to look a whole lot older. Or at least smaller.

"Nice trick," Sanders noted, from the front seat.

"Not that it'll fool anybody," she murmured.

"At a quick glance, it will," Sanders stated. "How's your own ability?"

"You mean, *my tracking*? I'm not a tracker at all."

"You may be, but all you've been doing so far is telepathy," Sanders pointed out. "Maybe you could recognize the energy of whoever out there is tracking us and give us a heads-up."

"Even if I could, what good would that do? I can't scramble his signals."

At that, Riff looked at her. "Are you sure about that?"

"No, of course I'm not sure. I've never tried anything like that."

"Exactly. If ever we had a time to see if it would work, we would really appreciate you trying it now. We could really use any advantage we can get."

She frowned at that but sagged back against the seat and closed her eyes. She tried to remember the little bit that Sanders and Terk had told her about keeping her energy calm. Not knowing what she was doing or if this was a time to keep her energy calm or not, she opened up the little bit of a window that she had into her telepathic ability and muttered to Sanders in the front seat, "Since I have a link to you that's well established, I'm not sure how this will affect you."

He responded, "Don't worry about it. You do you."

She had to laugh at that, or she would have if the circumstances weren't so dire. But she understood what he meant and closed her eyes, reaching out and looking for the tracker. If she could contact him, she knew she couldn't stop him from doing what he was doing because he was part of her father's team, but, if she could get his signature ... At that, another voice broke into her head.

That's an excellent way to do it, Terk noted, *if you think you're up for it. Also remember to stop him dead in his tracks from following you back because he's also looking for you. Therefore, his energy will try to glom onto yours, as well.*

She understood that. Most of that. *But how do I stop him from following my energy back?* she whispered.

If he locks on, you'll have to find a way to shake him off. I'm not sure what that'll take in this case, but it's really not negotiable. Otherwise he'll have your energy signature. If he can get locked on your position by following you, then everybody around you will be in danger.

Great, she muttered. *So maybe this isn't a good idea at all.*

It's a wonderful idea, ... if you can pull it off, he replied warmly. *Kudos to you for trying.*

Yeah, but, if I screw up, it'll be way worse for everybody.

We'll deal with that if it happens, but, if you can throw him off, then maybe you can get away this time, without his finding you.

She could only hope so. She closed her eyes and reached out to whoever was tracking her, and when a soft, almost shocked voice called out in her head, Ania smiled.

A man called out, *Who is that? What are you doing?*

I'm not doing anything, she murmured. *You are. You're the one who's hounding me to death, tracking me, making my life miserable, and for what? Helping my father to keep me a prisoner?* She felt his shock that she could reach out to him. *Just think when my father finds out that you couldn't even hide from me,* she noted, with a laugh. *You'll be much better off telling him that I have no skills at all.*

I don't dare do that. He already believes you have skills.

How did he find that out?

First came a moment's silence. *I'm not sure, but I think from your mother.*

Such hesitation filled his tone that she truly wondered herself. *Maybe, and maybe not. Maybe somebody else said something. It doesn't matter.*

Of course it matters, he argued. *The fact that you even opened up to me, … I don't understand.* He was equally bewildered and worried.

You know what it's like to be hunted, she said. *If you didn't work for my father, your life would be so much different.*

There is no life without working for your father. You know that, he stated bitterly. *It's not as if I have a choice either.*

Yet you do have a choice, she said. *Maybe not a choice you like, but you have a choice. I have no choice at all. I'll either be a literal prisoner or a hunted prisoner. You could tell my father quite clearly that I don't have any abilities and that, even with all the tracking you've been doing, you haven't seen any evidence of my having any abilities at all.*

And yet you're talking to me right now, he declared in an odd tone.

Didn't you know you could talk this way? she asked him.

No, he snapped. *I've only been able to send out energy. Why is it that you can talk to me like this?* he cried out, almost in anger.

Maybe because I have to, she replied. *Maybe because you haven't given me a choice. I'm sitting here, trying to have a real life, and I don't want to be hunted. So it'll be up to you to tell my father that I have no skills after all.*

These skills that you don't have, as in the ones that you're currently using?

Yes, it's called lying. But it would also cement your position, as being the only one with these abilities. At that, she realized she'd caught his attention. *You haven't been thinking this through, have you?*

I guess.

If he brings me back, you'll have to give up some of that cachet regarding being very good at what you do, she explained. *Because, if I can do this, who knows what else I can do? But, as soon as my father realizes that I'm better than you …*

Nobody said you were better than me, he pointed out.

Perhaps, but I found you. She laughed. *You didn't find me.*

But we did, we did find you, he clarified. *I can't always be perfect. None of us can.*

Of course not, but you would get an awful lot more time to develop and to hone your skills if you were … the one.

You're just trying to make me give up on you.

It's to your own benefit to do so, she noted, *because you would continue to be his favorite, and that relationship would give you all kinds of extras in life. Would it not?*

Of course. Of course it would, but I can't just lie to him. He would know.

Not particularly, if you ask me. I have known him much longer than you, and he may be good, but he's not that good, she murmured. *He's just frightening, so people crack.*

Why do you not want to come work for us? he asked in genuine puzzlement.

Because it's not pleasant for me. I have been detained in house arrest, and he's drugged me, and, even now, my abilities have suffered because of it.

Have they really? he asked, almost eagerly attaching to

her words.

Absolutely, and that's something he won't understand or at least won't acknowledge. That's too bad for him because it is exactly what he's done. He is responsible for this. Such a harsh bitterness filled her tone that he seemed to relax.

But your gifts can't be badly damaged if you're still doing this.

Yet they are, and I'm not able to hold this connection for long. So, it's up to you. What do you want for your life? Do you want to be his special pet who can do things and have time to work on them, develop them, and increase your skills? You know that if you can prove to him that you have better skills, he will do anything he can to help with your training.

Yet there is no training, he stated, as if he'd heard this argument time and time again. *There is no training that I can do to improve this.*

Why is that? she asked. *You really think you've done everything you can?*

Like you, I have also been given a plethora of drugs.

Silence. *The same drugs you fed to Sanders then?*

Yes, they used me as a guinea pig first. Then early on I decided it was better to work with them.

Of course. So you weren't the only prisoner being tortured and abused.

He hesitated, not sure what to say to that.

No need for you to lie to me. I've already spoken to Sanders.

Is he okay? he asked curiously.

He's lost his abilities because of what you did, and that's a problem, she shared. *To him, it's like having his senses completely cut off from everything else around him.*

Yes, I had that feeling for a while too, but mine did come back.

His didn't, she declared. *Perhaps because you raised his drugs on a regular basis.*

We did. Not by my choice. It was your father's decision.

You know my father doesn't like to lose, but, if you're seen as the only one to have these abilities, you'll have increased opportunities and could win in a big way.

Until he finds out that somebody is better.

Yet you would have the time to enhance your skills and potentially be better yourself. Maybe more so than me.

He hesitated at that, as if still unsure.

I can't keep this up, she repeated. Her fatigue was real, and she needed to let go. She needed him to see that this would be his future. *It took everything I had to do this now, and it took other people's abilities to lead me here.*

Can they help you, these other people, to get your energy back?

No. But they have been able to give me a boost, so I could contact you. You have to tell my father that I have nothing he wants, she whispered, knowing her own energy was failing. *And now I have to go.*

Wait, he cried out. *We can help you.*

No. You did this to me. You and my father did this to me, she said, with tears that she did not fake because she had had so much heartbreak from all they had done to her. *I didn't deserve this. I didn't do anything to you, and yet you still did this to me. Now whatever I thought I might have is gone, including my mother and my aunt.* And, with that, she quickly shut down the link.

She sagged back, feeling the exhaustion running through her.

But Terk's voice was strong in her head. *Now that was brilliant. Good job. It never even occurred to me to do that. You played it just right.*

She smiled. *Did I though? I don't know if he believed me.*

Even if he didn't, you've given his mind something to consider, something that may make this easier for him, if he really was the only one … And Terk's voice trailed away.

If he's the only tracker, he will do much better if he can convince my father that he's special and that he's the only one and that it was my father drugging me that cost me my abilities. That way, maybe anybody else my father gets his hands on will have it easier in that regard at least.

Of course. He'll also be much better prepared, more assured, for your father will take more prisoners, won't he?

Depends on if they can find anybody else with gifts, she noted, with a laugh. *I get that you seem to think a lot of us are out there, but I sure as heck haven't ever found any. The only one I ever had any contact with over here is Sanders.*

Of course, Terk murmured. *Yet I have quite a team, and there are lots of us, and I know there are more the world over. Maybe not lots, certainly not even one percent of the population, probably far less,* he admitted. *I don't know what the actual numbers would work out to be, but that isn't important. What matters is making sure that those who need help get it.*

She nodded slowly. *I'm ready to help with that, though I'm not exactly sure what I can do.*

You do realize that you just reached out to him telepathically, knocked on his mind, even though he didn't know who it was or why you were there, right? And he had no defenses against your ability to talk to him. That ability is something I can always use. Because, if you can do it in that vehicle, while you're driving through town, he pointed out, *you can do it from anywhere, even from here.*

Does that mean I get to stay at the castle and not do all these trips? she asked. *Because I don't think I'm cut out for this.*

You might not be cut out for it, Terk noted, *but you're doing a damn fine job. Don't worry about any of that now. We'll figure out where you belong and what you'll do when you get here. There might even be time for learning other things, after you sort out all this damn paperwork.*

At that, she started to laugh. *Is it really that bad?*

No, it's not that bad, he corrected. *My wife has been trying to keep up with it.* Yet a note of humor filled in his tone. *But she's carrying twins, and I know that it'll go downhill very quickly. When I told her that you had an accounting degree, she got pretty excited, so you can imagine how well she's enjoying and anticipating your arrival.*

Ania smiled. *Tell her that I'm on my way, I just don't know how long it'll take to get there.*

Oh, I've already told her, Terk shared comfortably. *No worries. We'll get you here, safe and sound. Just keep the faith.*

"WE'VE GOT COMPANY," Riff noted suddenly.

Sanders straightened and nodded. "Same vehicle as before?"

"Yeah. The airstrip's not too much farther ahead."

"Will we make a run for it?" Sanders asked.

"Oh, I suspect we will," Riff replied. "The problem is that I don't know if the pilot's aware of just how dangerous our approach will be. I don't want them to take out the pilot just because he's helping us."

"So, abort again?" Sanders asked, looking behind him to see Ania, curled up, sound asleep.

"It's not ideal, but if it's necessary, … we may have to. I

don't want to get the guy killed."

"Yeah, I agree," Sanders replied. "If we could slip through one of the open borders and steal a car on the other side, that could be a workable plan C," he murmured. "I think we'll have to take it."

With that, Riff swerved suddenly and headed down some backroads away from the airstrip, and Sanders felt his heart sinking, knowing without a doubt that their plan to fly out of this airstrip would not work.

"Better wake her up," Riff ordered.

"You don't have to," she muttered. "I'm here, very awake since you started with those quick turns." She shook her head. "What's the problem?"

"The problem is that we're being followed, and we're too close to the airstrip," Riff explained. "Being that close, we have to ditch that plan."

She groaned. "Dang, and here I thought we were so close this time."

"Close but no cigar, as they say," Riff shared cheerfully.

"Where are we going now?" she asked, looking out the window. "Good God, it's like we've stepped into into a horror movie. It's too dark out here."

"Yep, but we're really close to the border," he stated. "So, if we could get across at one of these open points in the backwoods, we can come out on the other side and carry on."

"Without a vehicle?" she asked.

Riff laughed. "Do you seriously think I can't get us another vehicle?"

She flashed him a grin. "I've learned a lot on this trip, and that is a skill I may need to learn myself."

"You absolutely should," Riff agreed, with a shrug. "Anybody who gets into the kind of troubles that you do definitely needs any advantage you can get."

She was left gasping at his instant retort, but she had no time for a comeback, as they were tossed from side to side, while Riff drove through the bushes at top speed. "Good God," she muttered, "how can you even see out there? It's pitch-black, and you don't even have the headlights on. We could hit a tree and crash any second now."

"Yeah, well, ... remember how I live in the shadows?" Riff asked her. "I can see out here just fine."

At that, Sanders blinked, staring at Riff in wonder. "Now that would be a very good skill to have," he muttered.

"And you can probably learn that one too," Riff suggested. "All this takes is some time, and you must have a chance to get to a place where you can unwind, recover, and learn this stuff, which is, as you know, what we're all rooting for."

Then, just as suddenly, Riff pulled to a stop in a pile of thickets. "Everybody out. Move it, people. I mean *now*."

Very quickly, she was out the door, shivering in the darkness, as Riff shut down the vehicle and pointed. "We're going in that direction, so stay close. If you get lost, just keep going forward. We should be able to tell you if you're losing your sense of direction."

"Says you," she huffed. "I have the sense of direction of a gnat."

He grinned. "This will be another chance for you to test out your abilities then."

She groaned at that. "Yet how come it's draining me to the point that I'm really struggling to use them?"

"We can discuss that later," Riff replied, as they raced forward, "but, right now, you don't have time. Do what you can to ensure you're not being followed, and I'll find you guys in a few minutes." And, with that, he quickly disappeared into the shadows again.

She swore, even as Sanders grabbed her hand and whispered, "Come on. Let's go."

"How does he just disappear like that?"

"I'll say it's a part of his charm," Sanders quipped, a note of laughter in his tone. "But it's also a talent, one I would really like to learn myself," he muttered. "He may not be the friendliest guy I know, but he's definitely got the skills when you need them. In my book, that's worth everything."

She wouldn't argue with that. Sanders may not have night vision like Riff had, but Sanders could see just fine in the moonlight.

He urged her on a bit faster. "The vehicle will have stopped and has probably found ours by now," he shared, "so we need to stay ahead of them."

"Says you," she muttered, stumbling behind him. "If they've gotten this far, what are the chances they'll find us, just like Riff managed to find this location."

"Probably depends on your father's tracker. If he's any good, then I guess they might find us. If he isn't, then he probably won't," he muttered. "So, we have to just hope like hell he's not that great."

At that, she added, "Oh, in that case, I should tell you something." Then she proceeded to tell him about her telepathic conversation with her father's tracker.

Sanders studied her intently. "So, you talked to the guy who's tracking us?"

CHAPTER 12

ANIA DIDN'T KNOW how long she and Sanders had marched in the darkness. "How do we know if we're going in the right direction?" she asked out loud for the umpteenth time.

He just squeezed her fingers and urged her forward.

She hated to say she was getting damn tired, but the truth was, she was getting damn tired. She wasn't sure how much farther she could go in the darkness like this. Yet she also knew she could go as long as she needed to because the alternative was to give up and to become a part of her father's twisted world once again. She was *not* prepared to do that.

When Sanders finally came to a stop, she bumped into him, only to have him grab her and whisper, "*Shh.*"

Immediately her senses came alive, as she looked around to see what had caused him to stop, and right there in front of them was a farmhouse, but it looked deserted. Or did it? She wasn't sure which this one would be. She didn't want anybody to get hurt or to get a jump on them. Yet they needed to get out of here, before they were caught.

As she watched, a vehicle drove up in the darkness and parked alongside the farmhouse in the driveway. Nobody from the house came out, and the driver of the vehicle didn't move. "Crap," she murmured. "I presume he's there for us."

"That would be my take on it," Sanders agreed softly. "I'm not getting any message, no indication that it's Riff, so presumably it's somebody else." Sanders held her back, gently pulling her farther into the shadows. "It could be him, or he might not be aware that we're already here," he murmured.

"But he would say something to us," she noted, her tone strong with conviction.

He smiled at her. "Riff probably would."

"Absolutely he would," she muttered, sliding farther back into the shadows yet again. "Regardless I don't trust it."

"Okay, good enough. Let's go up to the next farm then." She started shivering again. He wrapped an arm around her and asked, "Do you want my coat?"

"No," she said, staring at the vehicle. "I want him to go away and to leave us the car." Sanders almost chuckled at that, and she smiled up at him. "I sound like a two-year-old."

"Not at all. You sound like a woman who's been taken to the edge of her endurance and is being held there with no release in sight. But we're working on it, I promise."

"Seems that we've been working on it for a very long time now," she murmured, as she gave herself a headshake. "There I go with the pouty two-year-old routine again, and I'm really not, so let's just go. If it won't work at this house, we'll go on up to the next one. But wait. ... What's to stop him from coming up to the next one too?"

"I imagine he will go from here to the next one," he admitted honestly. "If I were hunting somebody, that's what I would do. I would have a man at each spot where they could be found. And one of your father's goons already told us that others are out there. So, we can either stay here and wait for him to leave, or go on to the next house to warm up. We just need to watch out for other men."

"I really don't want to go inside," she replied. "What if innocent people are in there?"

"Maybe there are, and maybe they would welcome a guest or three," he whispered, "but also there's a chance that the house is completely empty."

"I wonder if we have any way to tell ahead of time," she murmured, staring at it.

"You mean, like some sonar reading to see if anybody's in there, like a heat signature? That would be cool gift too."

"I don't know." She raised her hands in frustration. "But, if nobody is there, we could go in and rest for a bit."

"Yet if somebody is already looking for us and has stopped here, what's to stop others from coming too?"

"Oh, damn, you're right," she murmured. "Let's keep going."

Just then his phone vibrated. He pulled it out, read the text. "It's Riff, asking where we are."

"It's him, over in that car?" she asked excitedly, turning back to look at it.

"No, I don't think it is." And, rather than texting back, Sanders called Riff quickly. She listened with half an ear, as she watched the vehicle in front of her. It was obvious that it wasn't Riff, as the conversation developed a little further.

"He's one house up," Sanders noted, when he put away his phone. "He's looking for us, and we're to keep going along this fence line."

"Good enough." She suddenly wanted to get as far away from that vehicle as she could. "I don't like anything about the way it's just sitting there, almost as if it's waiting for us."

"He was probably hoping we would make that mistake,"

he murmured. "But come on, let's go." Then he quickly pulled her back into the shadows.

Moving swiftly in the darkness, with Sanders half carrying her, they came out of the brush at the next property, with her gasping for air.

"Sorry, but I wanted to ensure that we got away from that vehicle and hopefully find Riff, all before the vehicle got here to check out this location."

"Sanders, we can't outrun cars," she muttered in frustration.

"Wasn't planning on it," he murmured, as he pointed up ahead. "I would say that's Riff."

"Yeah, but how do we know for sure? Just because it's a vehicle at the second house, for all we know they have put several people in various different locations."

"You're right about that. Give me a minute. I'm calling him." He quickly phoned, and Riff answered almost instantly. "We're looking at a vehicle right now, but we can't tell if it's you or not."

"Flashing my lights for you," he replied calmly, and just then the vehicle in front of them flashed.

"Oh, thank God," she whispered, as they moved swiftly toward him. Just as they got there, another vehicle—hidden around the side of an outbuilding—turned on its lights and raced toward them.

"Shit," she said, bolting for Riff's car. They were inside and on the road within seconds, but the other vehicle was right on their tail. "That didn't go so well," she cried out, turning to look at the vehicle behind her. "I see just one man, the driver, and I bet he's pissed. Yet he was probably almost gleeful as he chased them. He's having way too much fun," she muttered.

"We followed a logical course of action, and that's the problem," Riff noted. "We needed to get you across the border, and, in that, we have succeeded."

She twisted and looked at him. "Seriously?"

"Yes, you are no longer in Estonia."

"Wow, who knew. Yet he's not acting like it's making a bit of difference to him."

"No, he isn't, which is also a bit of a concern because it should, unless he's been authorized by your father to take action on this side of the boundary as well."

"I would think so," she muttered, scrubbing her face. "My father has a very long reach."

"I'm sure he does, but, as it turns out, so do we," Riff added, with quiet encouragement. "Besides, we can lose this guy."

"And then what?" she asked. "Lose the next one and another one, then another one after that?"

"Unless you can convince them not to follow us or to find a way to stop them from coming after us, that's quite possibly the immediate future we have to look at," Riff admitted. "Once we get you over to Terk's place, you'll be much safer. But I can't guarantee that you'll be safe forever."

"No, nobody can do that." She sat back and sent another message to the man who had been tracking them. *Well, what did you decide?*

The voice in her head was angry. *You shouldn't have put thoughts like that in my head,* he cried out.

It just depends on if you want to be the hero in this instance.

He hesitated.

You know you can do it. If you tell my father that you had contact with me, that you checked me out, and that absolutely no energy came from my system, I'm sure he would believe you. Particularly since we're leaving for good.

But if I brought you back in and if we captured Sanders again, I'm sure I would end up being the one in charge anyway.

Maybe, but for how long? You know what he wants from me, and, if I give it to him, you know full well you'll be nothing but second fiddle to somebody else, just a footnote in his life, as he works with me instead.

He gave a scream of outrage.

See? You know I'm right, she declared, brutally pushing home the point. *All you have to do is tell my father that I don't have that energy anymore. That I don't have that ability.*

And yet apparently you do because look at you. You've contacted me again, he wailed, his voice barely containing what she could only assume was fury.

Maybe, she agreed, *or maybe you could explain that by saying how you tracked my failing energy in order to try and find us, but you don't have to tell him that I contacted you,* she explained. *You can make it sound like you're the one who made the contact. I'm just trying to help you out because, if I get brought in, … I'll let him know that you're completely useless and that I can do a much better job.*

He swore.

And you know I can, she said. *And I've just proven it. However, I don't want anything to do with my father or this life of his. That is your deal, if you want it. It's not for me.*

Yet it could be, he murmured. *You know that it could be, and you could become his favorite.*

I should have been his favorite anyway just because I'm his daughter. I should have been his favorite family member, Ania said bitterly. *Not his famous trick pony. That is something I don't need or want. You are welcome to have that coveted position.* When he hesitated, she continued. *Think about it. It could be the only way to save your skin, as we escape.*

You won't escape, he declared.

She had to wonder what that was about. *If you need to, use it to save your own skin. This isn't worth dying over.*

Not everybody has a choice about leaving.

For the first time, she heard that note of consideration in his tone. *No. But I am leaving, and I'm determined to survive. I don't want to take anybody else with us in terms of hurting them,* she pointed out. *That's not what we're about. I just want my peace and quiet. I want a chance to live without being a prisoner,* she murmured. *In your case you have a chance now to be somebody. You might as well take it. You might as well soften your position and do something to make your life a little easier.*

What if your father finds out? He will know that I did something.

How? You just tell him right now that the drugs must have damaged me, and it looks like I've lost whatever abilities I might have had. Then you can tell him how you checked on me a couple times down the road and still found nothing.

I wonder, he murmured.

You and I both know that the time to do this is now. Just send him a message and tell him that you've been trying to track us, but you're not getting anything from me or Sanders anymore. As if the drugs have finally worn off, taking our supposed abilities with it, and nothing you can do about it. And that's what you need to understand. There isn't anything you can do about it, and this won't end well. I'll do whatever it takes to survive and not be his pawn for the rest of my life. Whatever it takes.

And, with that, she once again cut the connection and

sagged back, tired and worn out. She called out to the front seat, "Damn, I'm exhausted. Is it supposed to do that?"

"Do what?" Riff asked.

She quickly explained what she'd just done.

Riff stared at her through the rearview mirror. "There are techniques you can learn," he told her. "The energy is all around you. It's a matter of understanding how to utilize it better, so it doesn't drain you. The fact that you're doing what you're doing is awesome. Just don't overexert yourself, so definitely stop doing it now," he suggested, with a laugh. "We'll need every bit of strength we can muster just to get out of here."

"And we still have somebody behind us."

"Yep, but not for long." As he quickly pulled onto a main highway, the early morning traffic was just picking up, and commuters were all around them. By quickly changing lanes and cutting through traffic, Riff had already managed to put several vehicles between them.

She turned around a little bit later and asked, "Did you lose him?"

"I think so," Riff replied, a quiet note of satisfaction in his tone. "I definitely think so."

She laughed. "And, if not, you're bound and determined that he won't come back again, aren't you?"

"Hey, we don't want to see him again," he muttered. "We don't want to see any of them again, to be honest."

"No, I sure don't." She twisted around once again to have a look. "I really don't see him back there anymore."

"Good, because we have a long drive ahead of us."

"*Great.* That airplane sure would have been nice."

"It would have, but we have to ensure that we're free and clear before we take anybody else into a dangerous situation," he stated calmly. "So, sit back and relax, and, with any luck, we'll be out of this in no time."

Splat!

That was all they heard, as the vehicle's back window shattered all over Ania.

CHAPTER 13

R IFF SWERVED THE vehicle to the right, yelling, "Are you okay?"

"I'm okay," Ania said from the footwell, where she was huddled. Sanders was curled up in the front seat.

"Stay down," Riff barked.

"So much for losing them," she muttered.

"Desperate people pull desperate stunts," Riff replied. "This is a sign that they're losing control. They're also in a whole different country right now, and that won't go over well, not for them."

"Sure, but we're also still being pursued, so it's unlikely they'll care right now."

"No, but they will very soon."

Almost immediately sirens came all around them, as the cops swarmed into the middle of this mess. Riff pulled onto a side road and then drove into the first alleyway he saw.

There Sanders hopped out, then came around and helped her out of the vehicle. "How are you doing?"

"Oh, I'm just great," she quipped. "That was absolutely the best thing ever."

He smiled. "You're holding up, and that makes you a trooper."

"I don't want to be a trooper," she whined, feeling suddenly teary-eyed. "I just want this nightmare to be over with."

"You and me both. I promise we're getting there."

She wanted to glare at him because, of all the things she had heard so far, that phrase was becoming all too familiar. And he knew that all too well.

He nodded. "I know. I get it, but we *are* getting there."

"You could have fooled me," she muttered, then looked around at the alleyway they were stuck in. "Now what do we do?"

"We'll sit here together, just the two of us. I am sure that Riff will come back with another car soon enough."

"Does he ever get tired of stealing cars?" she asked in amazement.

"He does it as long as we need to," he murmured. "And, if not him, it would be me, but nobody wants to leave you alone, while we go off and search for vehicles."

"Right, now I'm cramping your style."

He burst out laughing and then his laughter stopped as he turned her around. "You're hurt."

She stared up at him. "No, I'm fine."

"No, you're hurt. … You're bleeding."

Now she felt the stinging along her back. "Ah, crap, I'm really no good at the sight of blood."

"The good news is that it's on your back, so you shouldn't see it."

She gasped, twisting around to look.

But he turned her head firmly forward. "It's not a bullet, thank God. It looks like you've been cut from all the shattered glass."

"Well, gee, what should I expect?" As she went to shrug, she saw cops standing at the end of the alleyway, slowly approaching with their guns drawn. "Ah, crap," she muttered. "We have company."

Sanders stiffened and slowly turned and nodded. "Great. That's not exactly the way I wanted my day to end."

"Will they arrest us?" she asked fearfully.

"I don't know about arresting us, but we were shot at, and our vehicle was likely involved in some confrontation, so they'll want to charge us with something," he suggested, with a smile. He reached out his hands, showing that he wasn't armed, and called out a greeting.

As the first cop approached, Sanders said, "We were shot at." Pointing to the car, with the shattered back windshield, he then turned Ania to show him the bloody cuts on her back, now soaking her shirt. "We need help."

The first cop approached slowly and asked a million questions.

Sanders answered as best he could, and then Ania took over, as the cop was speaking Russian. Sanders let her do the talking because his Russian was a mess.

She explained how they were from Estonia and had come across the border this morning. They'd had somebody following them for a while. Then suddenly their vehicle was shot at. The cops fired off more questions, but the fact that she could speak the language seemed to relax them to some degree. She knew that helped and that they weren't the same guys who had shot at her, which was a relief.

When a cop car pulled in, and they were ordered to get in the back seat, she hesitated. The cop looked at her with a hard glare, as if to say that any arguments wouldn't be taken nicely. She got into the back seat, wincing as a piece of glass still in her shirt slipped across her shoulders, cutting her deeper. She gasped.

Sanders turned to the cop and said, "She's hurt and

needs medical care."

At that, the cop just nodded and thankfully took them straight to the hospital, but he didn't leave them alone. He stood by, while her cuts were treated. She felt tears in her eyes every time they cleaned the area, but there wasn't a whole lot she could do until it was done. Her shirt was cut and in shreds, but it was all she had, so she kept it, even though they tried to take it away from her. She looked up at Sanders. "Now I need a new shirt," she muttered almost mutinously.

He smiled. "That's the least of our worries," he murmured.

"Are they upset with us?" she asked.

"Of course they're upset. We disturbed their peace and quiet," he said, with a small smile. "But remember that we didn't do anything wrong."

"I know, but they're not exactly the friendliest, are they?"

"And again, something's gone wrong in their city, and they have us but nobody else to talk to, so we can't really expect great treatment."

At that, one of the cops turned, looked at the two of them, and asked, "Do you know who was shooting at you?"

This time the question was in English, so he had heard and had understood everything that they had just said. She shook her head. "My father had me kidnapped and drugged in Estonia." She provided the name of the city where he had held her.

He raised his eyebrows. "Why?"

She knew she couldn't tell him the truth. A discussion about her abilities wouldn't go over well. She shrugged. "I would love to know that myself, but, ever since my mother passed away, he's been …" She frowned. "I don't know how to say it, but … not quite right."

He nodded. "It can happen."

"It definitely can happen," she stated bitterly. "It did happen, and I don't know how to stay safe from him. He's high up in the government, and nobody there will help me. I left to get away from him, and then they shot at us."

Since it was the truth, she didn't even have to try to convince him of it, and she knew that it came across clear and easily.

"I'll get a statement from you, but I'll need names and details, so we can follow up."

"Of course he'll tell you that I'm off my medication and that I'm a danger." And she raised both hands. "All I can tell you is that everything was fine while my mother was alive. I have a degree in accounting. I'm heading to a job in England, and he decided that he wouldn't let me go."

The man was busy taking notes. He turned and looked at Sanders. "And your part in all this?"

She looked over at Sanders and shrugged. "He's going to England with me," she replied. "Of course my father doesn't approve." Considering love caused fights within families all over the world, she figured that would have a ring of truth to it, plus she didn't want Sanders to try to explain what had happened to him either. Talk of their special gifts or abilities wouldn't go over well, no matter who tried to explain it. She wanted to keep the story as simple and as clean as she could. Sanders didn't say anything else and just waited for more questions, but the cops were busy writing down everything they'd said so far.

When the cop reviewed his notes, he shook his head. "I need to go down to the station. I want you to stay in town, and you'll need to get that back cleaned up. Maybe get some clothes, and, while you are at it, I need to know where you're staying tonight."

"We'll catch a hotel then," Sanders replied. "We were just driving, not causing trouble in your beautiful city," he murmured, "but the shooters stopped us."

"Do you have insurance on the car?" the cop asked absentmindedly.

"Yes, but, of course, it's in Estonia. I'll phone them as soon as we're done here."

The cop nodded, but didn't say anything.

Ania immediately realized that their vehicle had been stolen, and, once the police found that out, it would be hell to pay. She stiffened.

Sanders grabbed her hand and squeezed it, adding, "You need some painkillers for your back."

The cop stepped away and, with a wave of his hand, said, "Go ahead. We'll handle this, but I need to know where you're staying tonight." He handed Sanders a card. "As soon as you find a place, contact me, at least by text, and let me know where you are. I don't want to find your bodies in some rundown hotel in a couple days because nobody checked on you." And, with that, he was gone.

Ania was allowed to leave a few minutes later, with a couple painkillers in her system and a prescription for more, if she needed them. As she walked out with Sanders at her side, she murmured, "You know I didn't want any painkillers, right?"

"I understand," he told her, "and, if it were that easy, I would be all over it, but that's a pretty impressive series of cuts on your back."

"Maybe," she murmured. "However, I would just as

soon not have any more drugs in my system.”

“Then let’s see how you do when the first drugs wear off. We can always fill the prescription and not use it.”

She wasn’t sure if that would even be necessary, but it might be good to have them if she needed them. She just hoped she wouldn’t. The last thing she wanted to deal with was more meds in her system. “It’s really just the side effects that bother me the most,” she murmured. “Absolutely nothing is nice about any of it.”

“Of course not, but sometimes, when the pain is too bad, there’s really no point in trying to fight it, as your body needs rest in order to heal.”

“I won’t be using my skills for anything right now,” she shared, “so, if my father’s tracker does try to contact me, he can’t reach me because I’ve shut everything down. Yet it will validate my story about losing my abilities,” she noted, with a snort.

“It all depends on whether your father trusts him or not,” Sanders suggested. “Also, if he finds out that he can’t reach me either, maybe he’ll just give up and let us both go.”

“I don’t know,” she murmured. “At the moment, I really don’t even care to think about him. Takes too much energy.”

“Let’s go. We don’t have wheels, but I think I saw a place not too far from here, where we can stay tonight.” And, with that, he made a couple phone calls and then smiled, nodding. “Seems we have a place to stay for the night.”

“Gee, and we didn’t even have to break in,” she muttered.

He burst out laughing at that. “I would give you a big hug for that bit of humor amid all your pain,” he said, “but I’m a bit concerned that a hug would hurt your back even more.”

"In that case, don't bother because it feels like it's on fire. After all our running and hard work, those sandwiches were a freaking long time ago."

"They were, no doubt," he agreed. "Let's get off the streets and inside for the night, and then I'll see what we can rustle up for a food delivery." And that's what they did.

About the time they got into their actual rooms, he looked around and nodded. "Now, are you okay if I leave you for a few minutes? A restaurant is just down the street."

"Absolutely," she murmured. "I'll go have a shower, try to ease the pain in my back, and then I might even crash."

"Don't crash yet, as the food won't be long." And, with final orders to lock up, he went out the door.

She quickly locked up behind him and headed for the shower.

IT DIDN'T TAKE very long to order food, and Sanders had ordered extra, just in case. He had no idea where Riff was but knew he would find them. That was another skill Sanders admired greatly, and it sucked seeing that these people could do so much when Sanders's own abilities were severely stunted still. But not for long, he hoped. He was really excited about the potential to have a legitimate opportunity to develop his skills, as everybody else in Terk's group was doing. Sanders just didn't have any way to know what that would take.

As he walked out of the restaurant with two large take-out bags, a guy was leaning against the building, studying him with a half smile.

"That's a lot of food."

"It is," Sanders agreed, without looking at him and walking past. "Game night with the boys."

That seemed to startle the stranger, or maybe it was the fact that Sanders spoke Russian with an English accent. He didn't know, kept on walking, deliberately not looking in the guy's direction, hoping he had nothing to do with this nightmare. But, as Sanders approached the hotel, he sensed the guy was walking in behind him. He turned in the lobby, gave the stranger a hard glance, and asked, "You following me?"

The stranger held up his hand. "No, no, not at all."

"Good thing," Sanders bit off, "because the last guy didn't do so well."

The stranger slowed and eyed him uncertainly.

"Yeah, that's what I thought," Sanders stated. "So, if you've got anything to do with this nightmare, I suggest you take some advice and run while you still can."

"Hey, I don't know anything about anything. It's just that word's gone out that somebody's paying for information."

"You could take the money," Sanders noted, "but I'll tell you right now that you'll never live to spend it. The guy paying this money has already tossed several of his men into the soup. He doesn't give a crap about anything."

"Maybe you could explain what the situation was."

"What's to explain?" Sanders asked. "It's a father looking to keep his daughter contained and drugged, like he kept her for the last several months. And, if you think that isn't sick, something is wrong with you."

The other man stepped back, his face twisting. "That's what he wants the information for?"

Sanders nodded. "Yeah, that's exactly it. They shot at us,

and the cops are already on the case," he added. "So you'd better hope they don't ask me about your presence because you're already standing in front of the cameras up here. Thus it will be pretty easy to identify you. So, if anything happens to us, just so you know, the cops will be all over you."

The stranger studied him, then saw the cameras pointed at his head and looked physically stunned. "I'm not … I'm not trying to cause you any trouble."

"In that case, get lost," Sanders snapped. "Don't tell him where we are because, if anything happens, it'll all come down on you."

The stranger shook his head. "I want nothing to do with it," he replied, trying an apologetic tone. "My own father was an asshole. So the last thing I want to do is cause some woman who's already suffered more trouble."

"Then go and don't bother even thinking about passing on any information because the repercussions for you will be costly."

With that, the stranger quickly left.

Sanders was sore, tired, and moving slowly, wondering about their options right now, as he stepped into the hotel room and called out, "Food."

When no answer came, his heart froze. He raced to the bathroom to find her in a bath, all curled up and sound asleep.

CHAPTER 14

ANIA MURMURED, AS her body was shifted, and the cold air hit her. She opened her eyes in shock, immediately struggling.

As she was clasped to his warm chest, Sanders whispered, "It's okay. It's okay. I've got you."

She sagged against him, only to realize she was dripping wet. "What happened?" she asked, as a second shock hit her. She was completely nude.

"You fell asleep in the bathtub," he explained, "and the water is quite cold now. So, if we don't get you warmed up, you'll risk getting seriously ill on us."

She blinked, trying to process the information. "I can't think of the last time I ever did something like that."

"It all goes to show you how exhausted you are." He put her carefully on the bed, covering her up with a towel and a blanket. "You'll sleep better in here." Then he filled her in on the events that occurred while he was out getting the food.

"Do I get time to sleep?" she asked, struggling with the news. "That guy followed you here and all."

"I know, but I think he got the message to leave us alone. Meanwhile, if you can grab a little bit more sleep, you'll be better off," he replied. "I just couldn't leave you in that cold water."

"Thank you for that." She yawned, tucked the blanket up to her neck, and carefully rolled over. "Maybe I will try to grab a few more minutes." She closed her eyes.

When she opened them again, he was beside her. "Did you even leave?" she muttered, blinking through the haze in her brain.

He chuckled. "I've checked on you several times. You've been asleep for close to four hours."

She stared at him in shock. "Seriously?"

He nodded. "Stop fidgeting. That's a good thing because, although I hate to say it, we need to get moving."

She groaned, closing her eyes, and whispered, "Now where?"

"Hopefully to a plane and home."

"In that case, I'm in," she said, sitting up and pulling the towel around her shoulders in an attempt to keep herself covered, which made absolutely no sense, considering he'd already pulled her out of her bath. She yawned again. "Just give me a chance to get dressed. Is there any coffee?"

"No, we'll pick up some on the way, or get some on the plane."

"On the plane works for me." As she shifted into a sitting position, she winced at the pull on her back. "What the hell?"

He nodded. "Remember the broken glass from the car? It's all been pulled out of your back, but you were cut up some, so it'll sting, and it's likely to be sore for a while."

"Yeah, I remember now. That's just great," she muttered, slowly rolling her shoulders.

"It'll be fine with a little more time."

It wasn't fine, but it was livable, and, if it made it possible for her to get out of here, then she was totally okay to pay the price.

Sanders pointed to a bag by the bathroom door. "Riff picked you up a couple things to replace your bloody clothes."

She nodded and slipped into the bathroom, where she dressed, gathering her bloody clothes into the now-empty bag. Then she headed out to the main room to see both men sitting there, drinking coffee. She glared. "You said no coffee."

He chuckled. "If you can call it that. It's pretty cold and bitter, but we're just a little more used to making do with it."

"Yeah?" she muttered. She walked over, picked up his cup, and drained it instantly. "Maybe you're used to it, but I'm not used to functioning without caffeine."

"It's all in the mind anyway," Riff noted in a mild tone. She turned and glared at him, and he smirked. "Yet, it is so much easier when caffeine freaks get what they need."

"Absolutely," she declared. She walked to the door and quickly put on her shoes, only to find the men already packed up and waiting for her. "We really are leaving, right?"

"We really are," Riff stated, with a smile.

"Any chance that we won't get followed and shot at, or God-only-knows what else this time?"

"Not much of a chance," Riff replied, his tone calm, certain. "But let's get you out of here, so we can sort out who might still be trying to come after us. How well do you think your brand of persuasion worked on your father's tracker?"

"Oh, I think he was quite intrigued, but I think he is worried about how he will prove it to my father. They are all so terrified of the man, so the prospect of being caught lying to him terrifies them. That's why they are so freaking loyal."

"Right," Riff agreed. "If we ever see your father, if he's

out here, having any part in this nightmare on a personal level, maybe you'll have a go at lying to him too."

"I could," she noted. "I just haven't a clue what I would even try to say at this point."

"Maybe don't say anything. Maybe that's all that's needed is for you not to say anything. If he's looking for answers and looking for you to be somebody other than you are, particularly if he doesn't really know how much of this is even real or why this would even be something that his own daughter could do, he might be easier to convince than you think."

"I don't know," she murmured. "Either way, let's just get out of here, so we're free and clear of whatever's going on," she muttered. "The sooner I'm over in England, the better. Surely MI6 or somebody there might convince my father that I'm not among his pawns anymore."

"Maybe," Riff said, with a nod. "Terk definitely has some pull in that regard. If nothing else, it might be enough to make you a protected citizen."

"I'll take that too," she replied. "Anything that would get this nightmare to stop. Nothing like being a prisoner to entrench fear in your DNA."

"We all understand that," Riff declared, with a hard smile in her direction. "We're all on your side. Now we just have to make it happen."

And, with that, they ushered her out into the hallway, then turned to lock the door behind him. They walked downstairs and then outside.

She immediately felt herself tensing up. "It's really hard to *not* consider that somebody is out here, waiting to shoot us," she muttered, a chill settling over her.

"Do you have any reading that is what somebody is

looking to do?" Riff asked, smiling at her.

"It's what's happened so far," she murmured, looking at him strangely. "If you're asking me if I'm getting any messages along those lines, I really don't have anything to tell you."

"In our business," he explained, "abilities or not, our instincts are everything. That has saved our lives time and time again, so don't ever discount it."

"I wasn't trying to," she muttered. "I was just trying to stay alive, though I'm not sure that's even a realistic expectation these days."

"It is, because we're getting you out," Sanders stated, taking her arm and leading her to the car.

It was a small and very low-to-the-ground silver car, completely nondescript, and yet something was odd about it. As she got into the back seat, she asked in an amused tone, "What are we driving? Any chance this is bulletproof glass?"

The men chuckled. "No, not at all," Riff replied, "but it is a street racing car, so, if we have a need for speed this time, … we'll have a powerhouse."

"Did you steal it too?" she asked in a joking manner. "Somebody will be pissed."

Riff, his grin wide, looked at her in the rearview mirror and shook his head. "I didn't need to. It was offered by somebody I know, who respects what we do."

"Nice to have friends. I don't suppose you told him what happened to the last couple vehicles we *borrowed*." She added air quotes to emphasize her point.

He just chuckled. "Actually I did, but he also knows the game and how it's played," he shared, his tone completely unconcerned. "So, don't worry about it. This friend of mine will hardly have a problem with any damage to his car."

"Well then, I don't know what kind of friends you have, because nobody I know has the money to turn around and pay for repairs on a rig like this," she stated.

"We have some friends with very deep pockets," Riff added, "and we have some friends who just like to be helpful. So, if this is a way that they can help out in a pinch, then they're totally okay with it."

She wanted to say something else, but they were pulling out of the parking lot. It was just instinctive for her to turn around and to look behind her, almost to say goodbye. Then she saw a man staring at them. "You know he's watching us, right?"

"Yeah, sure do," Riff noted, again in that completely offhand manner.

She glared at Sanders. "Why is it that you guys aren't bothered?"

He flashed her a big grin. "Because we do see him, and we do know that he's probably contacted somebody, but he's not trying to hide it, and that's an interesting thing in and of itself."

"Why?" she asked in confusion. "Why wouldn't he try to hide?" As she thought about it, the answer came to her all at once. "Oh, he's already told them, hasn't he?"

"He has told them, but that doesn't mean he's told them everything. We were pretty clear about the reasons your father wanted you, not necessarily in detail, but certainly enough for him to understand the scenario."

"But a lot of people don't care what we say," she stated, as she twisted to look back at him again. She was surprised to see that he was still standing there, his hands shoved deep in his pockets. "Do you think he did something to give them a different lead?"

"I think that he'll give them just enough to get paid but leave us a little bit of a buffer, so we can get out and away."

"But how will he know that you can make good use of that buffer?"

At that, Sanders burst out laughing. "He knows, and that is what he's counting on. At least he's done his job, and he's also out of trouble, so he can wash his hands of the whole thing, knowing that at least he gave us a fighting chance."

"Yeah, what if I want more than a fighting chance?" she muttered, hating to even think that she was still a pawn in somebody else's game. "He might think that he's out of trouble, but there are no guarantees with my father."

"And that's something that he'll find out for himself, one way or the other. He got into this, and now it's up to him to get himself out of it. Whether he does so in a healthy and safe way … is his problem. Your father doesn't have to know that he gave us a fifteen-minute head start, and, for one, I'm very grateful that he is giving it to us because, with that, we can be a long way away."

And, with that reassurance, she sat back and tried to relax, but she needed food. Almost instinctively, as she leaned forward, Sanders twisted around and handed her a bag. She looked at it in surprise.

Sanders said, "I thought maybe you would like the last sandwich."

"If I don't get fresh bacon and eggs in a fancy restaurant by the ocean, I suppose a cold leftover sandwich will do the job nicely."

His grin flashed at her, and he nodded. "I really like your attitude."

"Yeah, sometimes there isn't a whole lot of choice, is

there?"

"No, but it's how you handle the stressors in life that make the difference in how you move forward."

"Yeah, but I don't even know how I'm moving forward or what life after this will look like."

"I guess neither of us does, and, while both of us are heading to something new and different, I, for one, am really excited."

She couldn't argue with that, and everything he said was true. Up until now, he had been her lifeline, so she was willing to give him the benefit of the doubt. "I just hope that maybe we'll get there alive and well. Anything else looks to be a one-way street to a place I don't want to go."

"Don't focus on it," Riff interjected. "We aren't very far away from where we need to be, so we'll just keep driving until we get to our location. If we can't make that one, we'll go on to the next. We have three mapped out for today, and we have people ready and waiting at every turn," he shared, with a smile. "One even includes a private plane."

"You really do have friends in high places."

"The boss has a friend based out of Africa. He comes over and travels quite a bit, so that is his plane. Although it isn't well-known, it's certainly legal and registered in all these locations. And, if that's what it takes to help us out, he's right there for us," Riff explained calmly.

Pulling out the sandwich, Ania took several bites, hating the cardboard taste, but knowing it was better than nothing if she would have to run for it again. Just the thought of that exhausted her. She'd had a few hours of sleep, but it sure wasn't enough for a mad and crazy run again. She looked over at Riff and then at Sanders, wondering how the men had ended up in circumstances where this was the norm. As much as she wanted to ask them, she wasn't sure she really wanted to know. Yet she was so grateful they had come back for her.

"This won't be the only time I say it, but I just want you both to know that … I really appreciate how you came to help me out," she murmured. "I'm … I was doing okay, but I don't know that I would have been able to evade my father and his goons much longer. As you may have noticed, my father is very crafty when it comes to getting what he wants out of life."

"You don't need to thank us," Sanders replied. "You kept me alive mentally and emotionally when I was a prisoner, so I could hardly do less for you. I'm sorry it took as long as it did for me to get out and to rescue you. That wasn't quite my plan. I pushed it and got here as soon as I could."

"You don't look much better even now," she said bluntly. "So, you really owe a great deal to these women helping you out."

He chuckled. "One of them reminds me of that on a regular basis," he replied, with a smile. "But you're right, I owe them both for this, and I will be quite happy to repay them, as time goes on. I don't have any issues with that. Sometimes a good deed is not repayable in the exact same way, but I'm up for helping somebody else in whatever way is needed. Being rescued? … That's huge, but being able to rescue? That's even bigger," he murmured. "So, my thanks go to the entire team, … especially Riff here."

"Let's not go there," Riff muttered in an exasperated tone. "I can't do that whole maudlin thing."

She snorted. "Too damn bad. If we want to say *thank you*, we'll damn well do it, and you can just shut up and take it. I think I might even hug you." His startled look in the rearview mirror made her burst out laughing. "Yeah, I get the impression most people don't talk to you that way, but maybe they should."

"Yeah, and what makes you think that?" he asked, with a headshake. "Jeez, you let somebody into your life just this little tiny bit, and she walks all over you."

She giggled. "Hardly, and somebody like you is bound to be used to it, whether you want to admit it or not. This work comes so naturally to you, and you are so used to a lot of this stuff. So, you don't really see what a big deal it is to someone like me. It seems you were made for it, and you take to it like a duck takes to water."

"It's what I do," Riff stated firmly. "When the time comes that I don't want to do it anymore, ... I'll find something else to do. I have no intention of dying on the job, and I demand to live life to the fullest on the other side of this, whatever that is."

"Yeah, well, if you're hooked up with Terk and his group," Sanders replied, "apparently that'll mean a wife and babies." The horrified look he got in response from Riff made Sanders laugh. "Yeah, you may think that now ..." Sanders began.

"Yeah, and you know why," Riff declared, looking serious all of a sudden.

"I do know why. I don't know all the details, but I do know why," he said. "But I also know that you can't live in the past forever. At some point in time, that future will beckon, and it will be up to you whether you'll answer that call, or choose to be alone and miserable for the rest of your life."

She was surprised to hear that conversation, not knowing any of the details. As much as she wanted to ask, she had a feeling, based on the change in their tones, that her interference in that conversation would not be appropriate. Curious, but not willing to cross that line, she sat back and pondered it. Everyone had challenges and issues in their lives, so it was not surprising that Riff would have a few of his own as well.

It might also help explain some of his standoffishness. She could only hope that he found peace and quiet at the end of all this, because no doubt he was struggling. He may look put together, but he was exorcising demons of some kind. No matter how much she wanted to, it wasn't for her to ask, but, as long as he found that sense of peace at the end of the day, she would be happy.

SANDERS WATCHED THE vehicle pull up in the rearview mirror, looking over at Riff, who just nodded.

"I see him."

Sanders glanced at the back seat, but Ania was dozing lightly in place. "Do we wake her?" he asked.

"No," Riff said. "I'm hoping that we have a welcoming committee waiting for us when we get to the airport, with a little bit of backup."

"That would be good," Sanders muttered. "Any idea how they're tracking us?"

"Depending on how advanced her father's systems are, and what levels of the government he has access to, it could be any number of things," he muttered. "Once you start involving high-level government operatives, there really is no end to the information they can access. It's unfortunate, of course, because it would be a lot easier if we had an even playing field."

"We do have access to an awful lot, though," Sanders noted. "I mean, way more than I thought was even possible."

"That's because Levi has his own satellite, as does Bullard over in Africa," Riff shared. "They're both working to support Terk in the meantime, until he can get in the position of getting his own up in the air."

"Wouldn't it be better to just cooperate more instead of adding it to the cost?"

"Yes, but then you have all these wars raging around the world, and, as soon as somebody decides to take out one satellite, everybody's impacted."

That made a lot of sense, and, since there seemed to be money for it, redundancy could benefit them all. Now that Sanders had been one of the beneficiaries of such a system, he could only sit back and marvel at how much of the world functioned on a private level that he hadn't known a thing about. He watched as the vehicle just stayed on their tail. "I wonder if her father will come into this mess personally," Sanders muttered, "or if he will just stay on the sidelines."

"It depends. If the tracker has already told him that he doesn't think she has any abilities, then he might want to come see for himself. Not that he'll be able to read Ania for gifts, not when he has none himself. Yet, if he doesn't, he may always wonder if he had been taken for a ride. I would."

Sanders could only nod and agree with that. "I would too, and nothing quite like finding out for yourself whether somebody is lying to you or not. In this case, he doesn't want to lose something, but neither does he want to have all kinds of hell happen over it. This could turn out to be very expensive for him, and he could find himself called on the carpet over it."

"Exactly, and I would think that he's bound to be coming to that point soon. He isn't the president of the country, for God's sake, and somebody has to be watching what he's doing. The question is, do they understand what he's doing, not to mention how much in the way of resources he's putting into this? There are bound to be questions as to whether he's doing it on a personal level because it's his daughter, or whether he's doing it to benefit the country, or maybe a select group of people."

"But think about it for a minute. Can they really keep that completely separate?"

"They have to. Otherwise everybody would utilize all those resources for themselves over and over again, and it wouldn't benefit the government. Who'll pay for it? These guys don't have money rolling around for everybody to use, any more than the US or British governments will turn around and let us get all the stuff that we need."

"Yet we get quite a bit from MI6, I understand," Sanders noted.

"That's different. We work for them for a price, maybe not strictly paid in currency," Riff added, with an eye roll. "And while this job isn't one of MI6's, we've just come off several that were. One was where they lost their own people in transit."

"Lost?" Sanders repeated, turning and looking at him.

"Lost, as in they were recaptured by the countries that they were running away from," he muttered. "It got particularly ugly here recently, where a couple of their agents were killed too. So MI6 owes us. Thus any money that we spend, or any of their resources that we utilize for what we need, I don't have a problem with. But you are right about Terk. It's good that he has these kinds of mutual relationships."

"Exactly."

Just then Riff swore. "Hang on," he cried out, as the vehicle from behind slammed hard into the back of the car. He turned the car, just as Ania let out a terrified scream, right when Sanders reached for her hand.

"Hang on," Sanders explained. "We've just been found again, and they're trying to ram us off the road."

She just blinked, staring at him in horror.

"It's okay. Stay calm. We'll get out of this."

She nodded slowly, taking a deep breath. "This is just unbelievable. Why won't he just give it up? Why is it so important to get to me if he kills me?"

Such pain took over her facial expression that Sanders's own heart ached for her. "Either your father will go to great lengths because he wants to control you, or he'll go to great lengths because he's afraid to lose whatever it is that you represent," he explained. "But, at some point in time, even his bosses will get pissed off at him and will start asking hard questions."

At that, she looked at him, blinking owlishly, and then slowly nodded. "That could be why he's so adamant right now. He's gone down this pathway, and he's committed a lot to the task. So, if he doesn't have something to show for it at the end of the day, it could go badly for him. That makes a lot of sense, and he could end up getting in quite a bit of trouble himself," she noted softly. "When he's up against a wire like that, there is no give in him."

"He's not alone. A lot of people are like that," Riff declared, trying hard to shake the tail.

Just then the vehicle took another hard hit, and she lurched to the side. Yet Sanders still clung to her hand.

"We will get out of this," Sanders stated firmly.

"Yeah? Is that your telepathy telling you that?" she asked, with a laugh. "Because the fact that we can talk to each other mentally really doesn't cut it in this situation."

"No, that's quite true. You talking to your father's tracker may have helped though, but we can't see the results of that yet," he added, looking around. "I'm not sure what to do," Sanders told Riff, "but, if you have any ideas, feel free to tell me."

"Yeah, maybe you should tell me what you are able to do, since I have no idea."

"So, tell me what you would want in an ideal world," Sanders suggested, "and let me see if I can figure out how to make it happen."

Riff shot him a look and declared, "Get these assholes off our back."

Sanders turned and focused his attention on the vehicle on their tail, realizing that it was big and that it was strong. Yet Sanders felt something inside him that he had felt a couple times before, during the testing he had gone through in captivity. Back then he had struggled to keep his response dampened down. It was an anger beyond anything he had ever experienced. He felt that same fury now that somebody would do this to them, when they were so close to freedom, that someone would try to take that away from them, from her.

Ania had been through enough already, so why the hell wouldn't these guys just stop and let them go? Even though Sanders knew what was driving the goons, it wasn't enough. It would never be enough because they wouldn't let it be enough.

Sanders closed his eyes, and that same anger swirled inside him, and he stoked it, trying to build it up, when Terk popped into his head.

Stop. Don't use the anger.

What?

You'll regret it later. Stay detached from the anger, but use that energy that has been building up. Give that energy as much force as you can, Terk said. *I'm not sure what you can do with that energy, but, if you need more, we're right here. Just set aside the anger.*

Intrigued at the instruction, Sanders took the energy, gathered it together to create a sphere, and swirled it around.

That's right, Terk replied. *Yes, focus on getting that vehicle off your back.*

Sanders closed his eyes, his energy directed behind him, and he kept boiling up the energy, churning it faster, faster, until he almost had this fiery ball at his disposal. He opened his eyes, then turned and stared at the truck behind them. Sanders focused on one tire, and then mentally, with as much force as he could, he shot that fiery churning energy at the tire and watched in disbelief as the vehicle flipped over backward and came down flat on its roof, the wheels spinning in the air. His jaw dropped, and he watched in disbelief. "Good God," he cried out.

Ania twisted, looked at the vehicle behind them, then turned to him and over to Riff. She took another look behind her, amazed, then back to Sanders. "Did you just do that?"

"I don't know. Riff told me that we needed to get him off our tail, and I started to ..." He looked down at his hands. "Then Terk told me to try to ..." He sank back into the seat, frowning at Riff.

Riff's eyebrows were still raised, totally surprised, as he

looked at him. "Sanders, what the hell? If you'd told me you could do something like that, it could have come in handy before."

"I didn't know I could do that, and I'm still not sure I did," he admitted. "Terk was somewhere in the back of my brain."

"Terk's good at that," Riff noted. "But the fact of the matter is, I told you to get them off our back, and somehow that exact thing happened, and you're the only one who was facing the car behind us," he pointed out, looking at him several times, his gaze going from the road to him and then back again. "So, if you did do that, well, hot damn, we really do need you at home."

"I don't even know what the hell that is, what I just did, if I even did that," Sanders admitted in confusion.

Terk's laughter rolled through his head. *We don't really need to do a post-mortem right now,* he shared. *Just be ready in case another vehicle comes your way,* he added, with a smile evident in his tone.

Did I really do that? he asked. *I can't say it's anything I have ever attempted before.*

But you were never in a position where you needed to either, Terk noted gently. *I'm not here to tell you that we need to kill people or to hurt them, but, when it comes to evading people who are out to hurt us,* he said, emphasizing his point, *we must use all the tools that we have. You just found a new one, and, for that, I'm really proud of you. Welcome to the team.* And, with that, Terk was gone.

Sanders sat in the front seat, still stumped, quite disbelieving, as he stared down at his hands. A chill ran up his spine, yet this warm glow radiated around his heart. He smiled at Riff. "For the first time, it seems maybe I'm not a useless slug after all."

At that, Riff looked at him in shock. "I'm not sure where you got that idea."

"Oh, maybe from being a prisoner for all that time," he muttered. "It really kills your ability to do anything, and then before that, well …"

"And before that you were recovering from an accident, where you had severe injuries to your back and your liver and your intestines. Did you think we didn't get a full medical report on you?" he asked, looking at him. "I get where you could have that sense of helplessness, that sense of not having anything to offer anymore, but you've just blown that idea out of the water—though you had plenty to offer before that, as far as I'm concerned. We just need to get you home and healed up."

"I think that's why I'm just sitting here, with a goofy grin on my face. Apparently I'm not completely useless," he said, with a laugh. "But who the hell ever thought something like that was possible?"

"Yeah, you need to meet the rest of the team," Riff suggested, with a smile. "We have somebody who can completely camouflage people around us—and buildings. Not sure that he can do it from a distance, though," he added, frowning at that. Then out loud he said, "Hey, Terk, we might want to consider testing that camouflage thing from a distance and see what, if any, range he has."

Terk's voice filled the vehicle. "That's not necessarily something he can do yet, but we are working on it. If we could do that from home, it would be a massive step forward. We've tested it a little, and he can do it on the grounds and in other parts of the building, but, so far, we haven't been able to expand that reach yet."

Riff chuckled. "Sanders, something like that is the direction this team is going," he declared, beaming with satisfaction. "That's how you know that you've found your place. It's people like us, people working and developing something that nobody else in this world even understands, and if they did? … They would be all over it. That's exactly what happened to her."

Ania leaned forward. "*Her*, meaning me?" she asked, with snort. "I am right here, and I can hear you."

"You are here," he agreed. "Now if you can do any of the shit that Sanders just did, fly at it," he muttered.

"I've never tried anything like that, but I sure as heck don't want anybody here in this country to know about it, even if I could," she stated. "My life would definitely be much harder."

"Not any longer," Riff murmured, as they drove onto an airstrip, "because look at what's up ahead."

And right there in front of them, a plane waited. "Oh, thank God," she cried out, as the vehicle came to a stop right beside the plane.

She got out, stretched, looked around a bit, and smiled. "I won't be upset to say goodbye to this country," she murmured. "Like, wow, it's been a rough couple months."

"You're right. It has been," her father agreed, as he stepped out from behind the plane, two men at his side. "If you think it'll get any easier from here on in, you're wrong."

He lifted his handgun, and, instead of shooting her, which was what she expected, he shot Sanders without a warning.

His face blank with shock, Sanders dropped to the ground right in front of her.

CHAPTER 15

ANIA DROPPED TO her knees, completely ignoring her father, as she placed a hand on Sanders' neck. His pulse was strong and steady.

He half opened his eyes, and his lips twitched, and he still had that pained smile on his face as he spoke. "Can't say I expected that one."

She felt the tears in her eyes. She glared at her father, who approached warily, his handgun out in front of him. "Is this what you do? You just fire to kill? It doesn't matter that he might die?"

"He was taking you away. Obviously he kidnapped you," he said in his fake, soothing tone.

She glared at him. "Obviously not," she snapped. "I don't want to be with you, and I wanted to leave. I'm not a prisoner with him. And I have no desire to be your prisoner again." She glared at the two men beside her father. "You know perfectly well that he keeps me drugged and locked up and that I want absolutely nothing to do with him," she cried out. "I've also got friends in other places, and they've put in formal protests for me," she declared. "We'll see how the Russian government appreciates you for embarrassing them over this."

His eyebrows shot up. "What are you talking about?" he cried out. "You don't have friends anywhere."

"You mean, you tried to ensure I didn't have friends anywhere, but you're wrong. I do have friends. I have people who care about me and who will advocate on my behalf."

Sanders grabbed her hand and squeezed it gently.

She looked down at him, the tears falling. Then she faced her father. "And you," she began, "I hate you. I want nothing to do with you. Even if you do succeed in forcing me back into your illegal little prison, you will never hold me. If I don't arrive in England on schedule, they will ensure that the Russian government hears all about it. It will be plastered all over social media. You will be embarrassed, and the Russian government will disavow having somebody like you in their employ. Not to mention these two goons," she added, snarling at the two men who even now stared at her warily. "Do you not realize your careers are over? Do you not realize what he's done and how many rules he's broken to try and force me back into his little prison?"

"You don't know what you're talking about," her father stated.

"Really?"

"That last change of medication really twisted your mind."

"What it did was allow me to see again," she declared, glaring up at him.

There was absolutely no sign of Riff, and she didn't understand that. That man could disappear fast, but she also had to hope that he would appear shortly. She wanted to stand up, yet she didn't want to leave Sanders on the ground, bleeding.

"Besides, your little boyfriend here isn't dead, but I can fix that."

"I'm sure you would try," she replied, staring at him.

"You managed to make Mother's life hell, and then you killed her, right? So, of course, you would like to make my life hell too, and kill me as well, when I don't do you as you say, right? You have absolutely no goodness in your soul at all, but hear me now. You'll have to kill me today, if that's where this is going, where I'm repeating my mother's life of abuse and death by the hand of her abuser. You can bet that this is being witnessed and shared on social media, and everyone will know about what you've done."

He started to laugh. "Do you really think that anybody can see what we're doing here? I'm not such a fool. Nobody has that ability. Not even you."

"Ability?" she repeated, glaring at him. "Right. Back to your fantastical, crazy-ass notion that I have some psychic ability. I don't even know where you got that from," she cried out. "Who made my life such a nightmare by putting that in your head? Ever since you decided that was a thing, you thought that your daughter might get you some kudos, or notice in this world, with some physic skills. Tell me, *Father*. Would I have gone to school to become an accountant if I had any such skills? Where did you get such a crazy notion? You would have had better luck trying to get water from a stone. It doesn't work."

He stared at her warily. "Your mother told me that you had them."

"She lied," Ania snapped, her tone flat. Yet her heart sank, as, somewhere along the line, her mother had betrayed her, whether it was willingly, knowingly, or not. She shook her head. "And what did you do to her to get this false confession, *Father*? Threaten her, threaten me, beat her up? What, *Father*?"

He glared. "She mentioned something, and, when I

questioned her about it, she didn't know what to say, and she blurted out that you could talk to people in their heads. She told me that you had other abilities and that she didn't even know what all you could do. All she wanted was to ensure that you were looked after," he explained smoothly, "protected, because obviously you would be a danger to yourself and to others."

Ania started to laugh at that. "You're the one who's a danger to everyone around you." She snorted. "You lie, you cheat, you steal, and you kill … indiscriminately. You killed my mother. You killed my aunt. You're the only danger around here. The government lets you do it, which is a sadness in the world where we exist, but that doesn't mean it will always be so. You got away with making my mother's life miserable, my life miserable, then taking my mother's life," she stated, glaring at him, never hearing him disagree. "But I am no longer alone. I am no longer someone for you to abuse simply because you can," she snapped, then continued.

"Bully for you for picking on helpless females in this world, but this world is slowly waking up to who you really are and all the nasty crap you do," she declared. "It will not last. Even now news outlets are getting these reports about everything you've done, everything you've tried to do, everything you're responsible for doing," she proclaimed with such a fury and a confident finality that even her father looked rattled for a second.

"After killing my mother, you took away my cell phone and my laptop and burned my journal, and you kept me drugged, trying to control me, trying to cut me off from the world. … I managed to use a tablet, got online, and began working through my grief, making friends all over the world.

Throughout this last week, I've been posting all my latest *adventures* online. I have a global network of over one million followers, mostly women, who will see to it that my story is told. I also posted a photo of you and some of your goons, so the authorities arrest the right men."

She sneered at his two goons, staring at her in worry. "You have no idea how far off the reservation my father has gone, have you? How he's gone power-mad, taking government money for his own purposes. He will not survive this humiliation, this theft of Russian funds," she stated, glaring at the two men standing beside her father. "As he goes down, so too will you."

They looked over at her father, who stared at her with a fury that she'd never seen before. She stiffened, even as she called out telepathically to Terk and to her father's tracker.

The tracker went quiet for a moment, and then he said, *You're walking a dangerous path.*

I'm telling the truth. My father is a danger to anyone and everyone, but especially me.

Terk gave her an update. *Help is on the way. I don't know if you have any idea what's been going on,* he murmured. *But you're right about the social media aspect taking over. It's all been released. Your father's not big on social media, is he?*

Neither is anybody else in Russia, she replied, *but it's more prevalent here than it is at home.*

Once the police find out that he shot Sanders, that will be a whole different story as well.

No, it won't, because my father will just get away with it, again and again and again. It has to stop now, she said, almost hysterical, shaking her head. *I can't have him hurting anybody else, not because of me.*

She looked down at Sanders sadly and then spoke to her

father. "What you did to this man and what you did to me can't be allowed. There can never be more of this. It's not right, and you're not right. Something is wrong with you." She straightened and faced him head-on. "Maybe you have a mental problem. I don't know. Maybe the Russians need to do a full exam on your head and ensure that you get the same treatment I got," she suggested, with a laugh.

"Wouldn't that be ironic? To see you locked up and tested for the exact same things that I was put through. You are my father, as much as I don't want to acknowledge it. Yet, if anybody would have these abilities that I supposedly do, do you have the genes too? You would be suspect. That's brilliant. You should be tested and locked up, … exactly the same way I was."

"Stop this now," her father yelled, waving his gunhand. "Get away from him and get into the vehicle."

"No. You'll just make my life impossibly miserable, so you might as well kill me now."

He raised his handgun, his fury twisting his features, as he muttered, "Don't push it."

"I've already pushed it," she declared, steadily staring at him. "I've pushed all kinds of things these last few days, the last few months, but you know what I don't regret pushing? I don't regret pushing my way into the life of this man." She pointed to Sanders. "Into the world that you destroyed when you kept him prisoner, locked up like an animal," she cried out.

"And for what? For nothing. Just because you have some psychotic idea in your head that we have abilities, which you want to exploit for some godforsaken reason. Yet it's all a delusion, a delusion in *your* head. You're forcing us to play some macabre scenario here, dancing to your tune in order to create something that *you* can't create." She shook her head.

"I'm not doing it anymore. I don't know what you did to my mother to even make her tell you such lies, but I know she must have been desperate. And that's you, isn't it? You're the kind of person who beats up a sick old woman, so she's desperate to tell you anything just to have you go away. She even threw her daughter to the wolves because she had no other option. What kind of a man does that make you?" she asked.

"Or you, or you," she added, turning again to the two goons standing beside her father. "You're all sick people, who have absolutely no care in the world for anybody else. You are only concerned about what people can give you. You rule through fear. You are a terrible man. Worse, you're not a man at all." She was beyond hysterical at this point.

With her hands clenched at her side, she glared at the man who had dictated so much of her world for so long. He'd always rebuffed hugs and affection, much more concerned about what anybody could do for him, what he could make them do. After living in fear for so long, Ania was tired of it. She was tired of running, tired of not having real food or sound sleep. She was tired of always being afraid. She was tired of people hurting her and hurting Sanders.

It wasn't fair. She and Sanders hadn't done anything wrong. They hadn't hurt anybody, and yet here her father was, determined to hurt Sanders all over again, to hurt her all over again. No matter what they did, it just never seemed to make any difference. She straightened and took a step toward her father, feeling her fingers tighten into balls of fury that she couldn't even begin to control, yet she had to. Otherwise her father would just have more ammunition for everything that he wanted to prove in terms of her being unstable, how she needed medication, how she needed to be back under his care.

"You ignore the fact that I'm an adult, that I have a right to life on my own," she bellowed. "You ignore the fact that I don't want anything to do with you, that you're cruel and hurtful, and that everything you do is about power and control, with absolutely no sign of love or affection. You've got everybody else bamboozled into thinking that you care about me, and that it's all about looking after me, when the reality is so much worse. As usual, it has nothing to do with me, and everything to do with you and your own ability to coerce others to do your will," she snapped.

"You should be ashamed of yourself, but you aren't. You don't care. You believe your lies. But I do not. To think that you care, that you loved me or even loved my mother, is ridiculous. You don't, and you never have, and you never will." She took another step forward, feeling a certain satisfaction at seeing her father step back a little bit, as if afraid of her.

Maybe he was, and it gave her a sense of power that was almost addictive. In the back of her mind, she realized that very power was quite likely something that he felt every time he forced somebody to do something against their will, and she felt the same thing right now. But she wasn't him, and she wasn't like him at all, and never ever could be.

He was not worthy of even existing in this world right now, at least as far as she was concerned. She didn't want to hear any arguments either way on either side.

But when Sanders crept into her mind, he told her, *We all have to forgive, and the forgiveness starts with ourselves. I don't want you to do something to your father that you will regret for the rest of your life. You alone will have to live with that, so be careful.*

She stiffened, not liking the reminder, only to turn and face her father again. "You're lucky other people are here now, people willing to help me have a real life, so I have a place to go where I can be myself and can exist without you and the chaos you wield. People who are kind, caring, and generous. People who want me for me, not because they have an agenda."

Her father laughed. "Everybody has an agenda," Then he sneered. "Above anything else, that shows me that you are still such a child and that you have zero understanding of how the world works."

She shook her head. "No, it's not that at all. It's you who has zero understanding of how the world works. You don't have a clue what's going on. Leaving you in your ignorant bliss is fine by me," she muttered. "I just want you to leave me alone. What will it take for you to leave me alone?" she cried out passionately.

He shrugged. "You're coming back with me, whether you like it or not. If you have any skills, we'll find out," he said, his tone cool. "I don't particularly care what method we use to find out, but we'll take your lover here back with you because you'll behave yourself much better with him right beside you." He made a hand motion toward the two men at his side. "Go get him." Then he turned to Ania. "You stay put. I didn't kill him, but I still can," he warned, with a laugh, looking over at her, as his men walked to Sanders and reached down to pick him up.

She cried out, "No. You don't get to take him."

"Why not?" her father asked.

Furious at herself, furious at him, she stared at her father, not moving anything but her energy, and shoved that white-hot energy into her father's brain. Then she let loose into his brain the scream of telepathic fury that she hadn't been able to vocalize yet. He dropped to his knees, his face turning white, his hand going to his head, crying out in agony, as her scream continued to reverberate as loudly as it could, but only for him to hear, as she pushed all that energy she had available to her into his brain. And just as she realized that she was running out, more energy streamed through her fingers, through her head, and into his brain, as her psychic scream grew louder, longer, and harder in her father's head.

He stared at her in shock.

Amid her screams still ongoing in his brain, she yelled in that storm, *Goodbye, Father.*

He rolled up his eyes.

She allowed one final blast of her telepathic scream, and he collapsed to the ground, unconscious. She finally moved, turning to look at the two goons. "Touch Sanders and you die."

They both backed up and stared at her in shock.

She took a step toward them, and they both backed up even more, looking at each other, a flurry of Russian pouring from their mouths.

"What did you do to him?"

"What did you do to your father?"

"He'll kill you now."

Ania laughed. "Yeah, you're hoping so. Otherwise he'll come after you guys for failing him," she noted. "Pick up my father, get him back into that vehicle, and take him home, where he belongs. Did he just stroke out? Did he finally go so crazy that he now can't speak or stand? Whether he'll be a blithering idiot after this or not, I don't know. I don't care. But, if you or anybody else ever comes back after me or Sanders again"—she motioned to Sanders, still on the tarmac—"you will not survive it."

Such conviction filled her words, and, with the evidence of her own father, lying there, collapsed in front of her, that seemed enough to convince the goons. They quickly scooped up her father and backed away, shooting her hard looks.

One called out, "We could shoot you and kill you now."

She smiled. "Then do it. Right now. Do it, but you better not miss." she warned, walking toward them, faster and faster.

But then they screamed, racing for the car, shoving her father into the back seat, before hopping in and driving away.

She stood there and laughed. Even as they ripped past and looked at her in the rearview mirror, she lifted a hand and gave them the universal one-finger salute. Then she screamed after them, "Fuck you."

Almost immediately the force and the fury drained from her soul, and she turned, racing back to Sanders. She dropped down to his side, her hand gently stroking his face. "Hey, I think we're safe."

His eyes opened, and he looked at her, his expression dazed. "I don't know what you did, but, man, you gave me one hell of a headache."

She winced. "Yeah, I really don't know how to direct my telepathic rage," she muttered. "I don't know if I took some of your energy when I needed it or not. I wasn't trying to."

He squeezed her hand and said, "It's all good."

At the sound of slow clapping, she looked up to see Riff standing on the steps to the plane, with heavy artillery resting on the steps where he'd placed them next to each foot.

He lifted them. "I didn't even get to play with these toys, thanks to you, but, damn, when you figure out what to do with your gifts, you figure it out in a big way," he shared, with admiration. "I don't think those goons will ever survive, and now they must live with the fact that they ran away from you, like squeaky little mice."

She flashed him a big grin, feeling the success, almost euphoric, as she nodded. "I did good, didn't I?"

He grinned, leaving his toys propped up against the plane, then walked over and gave her a big hug. "You did better than good. You did awesome." He looked down at Sanders and added, "You, my friend, need to stop getting shot."

Sanders slowly made his way to his knees, and then, with their help, he got up. "Damn, I'm tired of taking bullets. But, in this case, I don't think they hit anything major."

"How could they not? You dropped like a rock. I just knew you were dead," Ania muttered.

"What else could I do? He shot me, and anything other than that would give me away."

She frowned at him, not understanding a word of it.

"He did get me in the arm, and I let it bleed all over my chest, but I'm okay. It'll take a bit to snap out of this one."

Riff efficiently ripped apart Sanders's shirt, took a serious look at the wound, and noted, "The bullet went through, and, though it's damaged some muscle, it missed the bone from the looks of it." He looked up to see how Sanders reacted and asked, "Do you want to see somebody here?"

But Sanders shook his head. "No, let's bind this up and get the hell out of here," he stated, not having any of it. "I mean, while I'm pretty sure they won't come back again, … who knows how many goons Ania's father had after us, and I don't want to take a chance that someone didn't get the latest memo," he muttered.

"Not that I don't want that too, but, Sanders, we gotta get you to a doctor," Ania declared.

Sanders laughed. "Somehow I think I will be okay."

Ania addressed Riff now. "What is he talking about? Has he gone crazy?"

Riff eyed Sanders, got another look at his wound, then nodded. "You're some crazy healer, aren't you? Wow. So maybe having the healing twins working on you transferred some of that mojo to you, or did you have this before?" Riff asked Sanders.

Sanders just shrugged, then winced. "You tell me. You guys are the experts. Yet it still hurts when I move."

Riff snorted. "Then don't move."

Ania frowned at them both. "Sanders is a healer?" she asked Riff.

"Appears to be. We'll still get him checked out." And, with that, Riff headed toward the front of the plane and asked them, "You okay if I fly this thing?"

They both stared at him. Sanders asked, "Do you fly?"

"I do," Riff confirmed. "I just wanted to know if either of you had any objection to flying with me."

"And if we do?" she asked him. "Then what?" Still, she climbed the steps behind Riff, helping Sanders navigate them too.

He shrugged. "I guess I could always hop out of my head and let somebody else fly."

"Oh God, no." She stared at him in horror. "Please tell me that's not a thing."

He burst out laughing. "In that case, I'll tell you that … it's *not* a thing." He entered the cabin and sat in the pilot's chair.

But the smugness to his tone had her staring in shock. She looked over at Sanders. "Surely they can't do that."

He laughed. "At this point, I have no idea what any of us can do," Sanders admitted. "Did you think you could drop your father to his knees, doing whatever you just did to him?"

"I'm not even sure what I did," she conceded, her tone soft, as she sat down beside Sanders and strapped him in. She looked at the wound in his shoulder. "When he shot you, when I saw all that blood—" She shuddered. "I just couldn't think anymore. Something else took over, and I went into overdrive. I went nuts a little bit, but in a good way."

Sanders nodded. "And I understand that because that is also why I came back after you, before I had any business even traveling, much less trying to rescue anybody," he shared, gently touching her cheek. "I couldn't leave you for another minute longer than necessary in the same hell I had just escaped from. No matter the risk, I just couldn't do that to you."

She smiled mistily. "You sure we're ready for whatever Terk's got in store for us? It's not as if we have the same skills."

He chuckled. "Maybe we don't have the same skills, but I think we've proven we have some."

She looked over at him and smiled. "I guess that's true, isn't it?" she said in delight. "Maybe we aren't quite as useless as we thought we were."

"No, I don't think we are," he agreed. "We just needed the right circumstances to force it out in the open. In my case it was knowing you were hurt."

"And, in mine, it was seeing you get shot," she added, with a nod.

"I guess that means we care, *huh*?"

She gave him a cheeky grin. "Although I won't be the first one to say it."

"You don't have to be the first one. I'll say it. I care. I care as much as I ever thought I could care about anyone. I honestly didn't even think something like this was possible," he murmured. "And, if we weren't here in an airplane, with Riff flying, which could be kind of scary, considering the way he drives"—he gave an eye roll toward the front of the plane—"I would take you in my arms and show you just how much I care for you."

She gazed at him, her lips quirking. "I'll let you off the hook this time, but, when you're healed, … you'll have a job to do."

"Yeah, and what's that?" he asked, his eyes alight with laughter.

"You'll show me, prove to me, over and over again, just how much you care about me."

"Yeah? Will that involve a bed and some time alone by any chance?" he asked, waggling his eyebrows.

"Oh, I think it should," she agreed, as she snuggled up against his good shoulder. "I really think it should."

SANDERS'S ARM AND shoulder hurt like a bitch, but having her curled up beside him made it bearable. It seemed like the plane ride took several hours, but he knew it wasn't that long. He dozed, got up, and walked around a bit, then dozed some more, and when they finally landed in England, he couldn't have been more relieved.

Slowly making his way out of the airplane, Riff walked down behind him and stated, "Now you'll have to get that looked at by a real doctor. We'll make sure it gets taken care of, what with your newbie healing skills at play here."

"I won't argue with that," Sanders replied, "and, after that, I'll need a few days alone to just chill for a bit."

"Will you do that on your own, or will you come back to the castle to recuperate?" He turned and looked at Ania. "Do you want to go to Terk's place first or spend a few days on your own?"

"Spend a few days," she said, "not to mention the fact that I have no clothes without blood on them again, and I need to sleep for a week. We'll hardly be in any shape to be social or even on our best behavior if we arrive looking like refugees," she noted, with a laugh.

"That's about what I expected," Riff said. "In that case, let's get Sanders checked out first, and, after that, we'll get you into a hotel."

And that's what they did. It took a good six hours before they were alone, with Riff promising to check in the next morning. Now with food already ordered, Sanders walked in and gingerly sat down at the small dining table. "We still need clothes."

"I know, but I figured, if you got a day's rest, that would help."

He nodded, but he still looked down at his clothing. "I'm covered in blood. I had a bag somewhere along the line, but I think we lost it."

"I'm not sure about that. Riff dropped something by the door." She quickly walked there and brought it back.

He smiled. "Okay, in that case, I should at least have a change of clothes," he said, looking coy, "and, if the food will be a little bit, … I'll go have a shower."

"Do you think you should?" she asked, looking at his arm.

"Yes, I need to. I'm filthy, stinky, and covered in blood, so, yeah, a shower would be perfect."

"I'll run the water for you." And she did, stepping in ahead of him and adjusting the temperature. "You need any help?"

He shook his head. "I should be fine."

"I'll need a shower after you, so don't use all the hot water."

"We're in a hotel, so we shouldn't run out of hot water that quickly," he noted. "If I were in better shape, I would say, let's save time and have shower together."

She stopped and looked at him, one eyebrow up. "Not a bad idea anyway."

"Why is that?" he asked, as he gingerly peeled off the rest of his tattered shirt.

"Because somebody needs to clean your back, and you can't twist or move enough to get anywhere close on your own," she stated, her hands on her hips, glaring at him.

He laughed. "I can try," he said, with a smile. "I need a nice long hot shower. I haven't been clean in weeks."

"I know how you feel." She yawned. "That's how I feel about sleep."

"You'll get sleep, as soon as we get some food," he promised. "We just need a couple more things to fall into place, like food and showers, and then we have two days to just chill."

He continued to strip down and stepped into the hot

shower, sucking back his breath as the water hit his shoulder. He leaned against the shower wall and let it soak in, knowing that she was right, and he could have used a hand with scrubbing, and he certainly wouldn't trust his own body to that extent. But when the curtain was pulled back again and she stepped in, fully nude beside him, he looked at her in surprise.

She shrugged. "You know I'm right." She picked up the bar of soap and got to work.

He hadn't realized how much of his chest, back, and arm were covered with crusty dried blood, but it took her a good twenty minutes to get it all cleaned up. He was more than happy that she did. "Thank you. The painkillers are decent, but they won't last forever, and I didn't want them to give out in here."

She just smiled and continued taking care of him, not with a completely neutral action, but definitely caring, yet he didn't feel like a child when she did it either. Something to be said for having a woman looking after him that way.

By the time she was done, he said, "Now you turn around. I still have one good hand, and your back could use some attention."

"Are you sure?" she asked.

He nodded and proceeded to carefully and efficiently clean her back, and then turned her around. "I don't trust myself to do the front though."

She smiled, then kissed him on his cheek. "This would not be the place to do what's on your mind anyway," she pointed out, "not with your shoulder like it is." She quickly shampooed her hair, then looked up at his and then added, "We should do your hair too, or you are sure to feel grody."

By the time they were completely done, he felt wiped

out again.

She nodded. "You look the way I feel," she muttered. "We're a hell of a pair."

"The good news is, we're not on any time frame anymore. We don't have to run around and hide from people, so we can take as much time as we need. … We have all the time in the world." And with a towel wrapped around his hips, he stepped out into the bedroom, just in time for a knock on the door. She froze at his side, and he smiled. "That is likely to be food service, but it could also be Riff."

He walked up to the front door, checked, and sure enough it was food service. He allowed them to bring the cart in, while he kept a wary eye on the man's actions.

As soon as he was gone, Ania stepped out of the bathroom. "And there's coffee," she cried out in delight, looking at the assortment arranged for them.

He laughed. "I did insist on coffee, even though we'll sleep soon. I figured you would want a cup anyway."

"Absolutely," she murmured. She quickly poured cups for both of them and pushed the trolley closer to the table. They sat together, still wrapped up in towels, and devoured a hot meal, their first in days. She sat back with a sigh of satisfaction. "What is it about hot food and just that sense of security in knowing that you've got food and coffee in front of you, all to make everything feel like it'll be okay again."

"In this case, everything *will* be okay again," he stated, with a smile. "So it's good that you feel that way." He picked up his coffee and moved over to the couch. "I'll enjoy this coffee, then I'll go crash. I have no more energy left in me. What about you?"

"Same," she muttered. She shifted the towel, still wrapped around her, and noted, "I don't even have clothes."

"There are robes behind the bathroom door," he noted.

"Are there?" she asked, looking at him. "You didn't grab one?"

He shrugged. "I didn't care about one and figured my shoulder would be better off without it."

She looked down at her towel, shrugged, and sat down beside him. "It's not as if we need to keep ourselves hidden at this point, I guess," she murmured.

"No, you're right," he agreed. "I don't know what beauty regimen you have, but, after all you've been through, you still glow with a wonderful light."

She laughed. "That just sounds like a man in love."

He froze, then he looked at her, his eyes wide. "It didn't even occur to me before this, but I think you're right."

She stared at him in shock. "Oh, no. No, no, no. You don't get to say that. Not right after what I just said. This is not how this works."

He started to chuckle. "I've never been in love. So it's never hit me before. It's not as if I've had time to even assess any of this," he murmured, feeling joy swelling in his heart as he stared at her. "But there had to be one hell of a reason why I felt so strongly about coming back and getting you right away," he noted, with a cheeky grin. "I kept thinking there had to be a reason behind it all."

She rolled her eyes. "What, because you love me?" she asked mockingly.

"It's definitely because I cared about you, about us. The rest just seems to have fallen into place over this past crazy week."

"It's definitely been crazy," she agreed. "I'll give you that. As far as the other, if you really mean it, you can repeat it tomorrow, when I know you're not under the influence of those drugs running through your system."

He chuckled. "That's a deal," He looked down at his empty cup. "If we push that trolley back outside, we can order more food when we wake up again in the morning. Right now, I just need to crash."

With a last bit of effort, he got up, loaded up the dishes, and pushed the trolley out into the hallway to be collected. Stepping back inside, he locked the door. "What about you?"

"I'm going to bed," she murmured, already yawning.

He nodded and led the way to the bedroom. Pulling back the covers, he said, "Hope you're okay with one bed."

"I'm totally okay with one bed. I'm looking forward to it." Then she curled up and pulled the covers around her.

As soon as he lay down on his good side, he pulled her up against his chest, being careful of her back then whispered, "This feels so damn right."

"That's because it is right," she declared. "Ours was not a normal path in any way, shape, or form, but that's okay because we ended up in the right place anyway."

He kissed her gently. "I'll see you in the morning." Then he closed his eyes and crashed.

CHAPTER 16

ANIA WOKE UP, wondering at the heat that surrounded her. It was like being tucked up against a furnace. She rolled over to see Sanders sleeping at her side, his breath steady, slow, and deep. She smiled as she gently slid a fingertip across his stubbly beard.

"I need to shave," he muttered.

She placed her finger against his lips and whispered, "It's not an issue. We haven't had two minutes to even breathe, let alone take care of basics like shaving."

He opened his eyes, and she was hit with that smoky gray look that fascinated her. "Those eyes, they're definitely deadly."

Surprise lit a light deep inside him.

She nodded. "Absolutely," she murmured, hugging him gently. "How's the shoulder?" She watched him do a quick self-assessment, then nod.

"It doesn't feel too terribly bad."

"Good," she declared. "I was good. I waited until you woke up at least." Then she pushed herself up on one elbow, leaned over, and laid a kiss on him that knocked him flat. When she finally lifted her head, he stared up at her, dazed.

"Wow." With his good arm, he pulled her down on top of him. "You can do that to me any old time."

She chuckled. "I was hoping that maybe you were

healthy enough that we could, you know, play a little bit."

"I am definitely healthy enough," he stated.

She gave him a knowing grin. "You'll be damn sore afterward."

"It'll be 100 percent worth it," he said.

She burst out laughing again. "I don't want you to hurt yourself," she noted innocently, "so we should probably hold off." But, as she went to pull away, his good arm was like a vise around her waist.

He tugged her gently forward. "Oh, no, you don't. You don't get to open up a scenario like that and then walk away," he murmured. "Absolutely no way. I've been waiting way too long." He kissed her gently, then not so gently. By the time he finally raised his head, she was panting with need, feeling out of her element.

"Good God," she moaned. "I don't know whether it's you or a combination of us, but holy shit."

He pulled her down and whispered against her lips, "How about more action, less talk? We'll do an analysis later."

"Screw the analysis."

His lips twitched at her remark. "How about you screw me instead?"

And, with that, she laughed out loud, then sat up, straddled him, tossing off the sheet and the blanket they had slept under, both falling to the ground. "Now that I can do." Touching him gently with her hand, she stroked the erection with wonder, as he responded and pulsed under her soft touch.

"You won't do that for long," he gasped, sliding farther up the bed to get away from her touch.

"Yeah, well, you started this, so now we'll finish it."

"I hope so," he said fervently, with a flashing smile. "But, holy crap, I won't control it very well the first time."

"That's okay. No pressure either way, especially if you won't be too long on the recovery."

"I have no idea how long I'll be on the recovery side," he admitted, moaning again, as her hands gently encircled him and squeezed. He quickly pulled her higher up on his body.

She sat back, only to find that he was in the right position. "Oh, that was tricky. I don't know how you did that, but that was tricky. Trippy too." She slowly sank all the way down on his shaft, throwing her head back and crying out as he filled her completely. Then she looked down at him, grabbed his good shoulder, and started to ride. He cried out beneath her, twisting, and she was afraid that she was hurting him, but the joy on his face, that mix of pain and pleasure, reverberated through her own body, making her incapable of stopping, and the tension coiled tighter and tighter.

She moved faster and faster, crying out, when he suddenly grabbed her hips with his one arm and slammed her down hard, as he lurched up beneath her. With a shout, she exploded in place, shuddering and feeling his own climax rippling through both of them. She sank down on top of him, careful of his shoulder, then smiled as she slowly recuperated.

"Now that was definitely repeatable."

"We might need a little more practice," she teased. "That sore shoulder of yours is definitely cramping our style."

"You know that practice is a good thing," he added, with a big nod. "I can see us practicing quite a bit. A hell of a lot more."

But then she asked him, "Do you think there's more

food?" When he smiled at her, she shrugged. "I missed a lot of meals."

He burst out laughing. "Absolutely, we can definitely get more food." He was still in a fit of laughter, when he asked her, "Now or later?"

She gave him a slow wink. "What do you have in mind?" she asked, waggling her eyebrows. "Because I would be okay to try this all over again. Remember the thing about practice?"

"Oh. I think we can definitely try that all over again." He pulled her to him and twisted her around, so she was beneath him, her thighs spread wide, and he was already sitting at the heart of her.

Her eyes widened. "Smooth move, slick," she muttered, now laughing too.

When he was suddenly deep in the heart of her, she shuddered and arched beneath him. This time the coupling was hard and fast, and, when she screamed in his arms, he ripped to his climax right behind her.

She opened her eyes the second time and muttered, "Good God, we'll need to order a lot of food if we keep this up. We'll kill ourselves this way."

"Yeah, but what a way to die." He leaned over and gave her a smacking kiss. "This time together right now is a gift, so I suggest we enjoy it as much as we can because, after this, we'll be part of a very large group of people where there won't be any secrets."

She winced at that. "It'll take a bit to get used to," she muttered. "It may take some time to find our own balance there."

"It will. But just think how they're there for us, and we'll be there for them. That makes a hell of a lot of difference."

She smiled, wrapped her arms around his neck, and added, "As long as you're there for me, I don't care about the rest. I'm happy to be part of a team, but I'm going there for you. Okay, maybe for me too, but it's you I want to spend my time with."

"That's a given." He leaned over and kissed her gently. "Now, how about we go order that food?"

AND THAT WAS the start of several days of relaxing and recuperating for both of them.

Four days later, Sanders woke up to a text from Terk. He rolled over, looked at Ania, and asked, "You awake?"

"*Uh-huh,*" she murmured, still tucked up against him. "Why?"

"Terk just texted me, wanting to know when we're coming."

"We were planning on today, weren't we?"

"Yes, he's just confirming."

"Tell him it's a go for today," she said. "I'm looking forward to it."

"I think he has a job."

"Not for us though, right?" she asked, her eyes wide.

"No, not for us, but we'll have to make our way to the castle on our own. Apparently Riff's heading out somewhere else."

"That's okay. We can manage that," she noted, looping her arm around his neck. "But we don't have to go just yet, do we?"

"Checkout's at eleven a.m." He looked over at his cell phone. "It's only seven."

She gave him a sleepy smile and nodded. "Perfect, we've got four hours." And, with that, she pulled him down and kissed him thoroughly.

T ERK SAT AT the table, his team growing and expanding by the week, it seemed. He needed to get one of those big-screen TVs, like what Ice had set up in her place for their team. It would be great for conference calls or Zoom meetings. He reached for his phone, selected a Contact to call, and put the phone on Speaker. "Riff, what's going on?" Terk asked. "I thought you were coming back with Sanders and Ania."

"They'll be there today," he replied, "but I got another lead on my fiancée's murder, so I'm taking off to do that." He hesitated a bit and asked carefully, "You don't have a job, do you?"

"I do, but it depends on where you're heading."

"To the US. The state of Maine, to be exact. I need to talk to an old friend of hers. Apparently, she spoke to him not too long before she died."

"You could call," Terk suggested.

"I know I could, but he's an old guy, not big on technology and really not big on strangers. Plus, he seems to have a chip on his shoulder about me."

"Ah. Do you want backup?"

"No, this won't be anything physical," Riff stated, "but I'll be over there. If you've got anything you need me to do while I'm there, you can let me know. I'm always available, but you guys could probably use some peace and quiet for a while."

"That's not likely to happen for quite some time," Terk declared, with a note of humor in his tone. "You know what the world is like."

"Yeah, it's a mess, and I'm damn tired of it."

"I hear you there," Terk murmured. "Who knows whether we'll get any calls for assistance or not, but, maybe after you're done, depending on whatever's going on, we'll move you to the next job."

"What's that?"

Just then Gage walked in, holding up his phone. "Bullard's been trying to get through to you, but it keeps ringing busy, so he called me instead."

"Hang on a minute, Riff," Terk said, turning to Gage and taking the phone from his hand. "Bullard, you still there?"

"Yeah, I am. I had a new nurse I was bringing over to see if she wanted to do some training here. She landed in Paris and was due to get a connecting flight after spending two days there, but she apparently missed the flight. I checked the hotel, and there's no sign of her. I think I should send a man over, but I'm spread pretty thin at the moment."

"That's fine. I've got some men who are available, and we are closer," Terk pointed out. "Is this a case of needing our particular brand of skills or just manpower?"

"I don't know yet," Bullard admitted. "One of the reasons why I was looking at hiring her is because she has a reputation for uncanny healing." He sounded almost lost in thoughts. "Although that's not necessarily a *your group versus my group* thing, I just thought I would check and see if she happened to have some abilities. You know how we could always use that here," he muttered. "Yet it seems as if, as soon as anybody finds out about your group, they head to you." He sounded frustrated. "I don't care if she goes to you or to me. I just want to know that somebody I feel responsible for is safe, and, so far, I haven't been able to raise her at all. We've done some basic research, so I'll send you the file. If you can give us a hand on this one, I would appreciate it."

"We got it," Terk replied. "Riff is heading to the US right now, so that won't work, but I do have somebody else I was looking at hiring, or at least at testing, so this might be a good opportunity for that."

"How about I send one of my guys as backup?"

"Sounds good."

"So you have another new guy who's doing your kind of work?"

"Maybe," Terk said. "He's not admitting to doing this energy work, but he's an ex-Navy SEAL who's been working out of Ireland for the last four years. I heard via the grapevine that he had some abilities. He's not against doing a job for me, but he certainly isn't being forthcoming about any unique skills I might be interested in."

"Of course not." Bullard laughed. "Nobody would because it'll make him sound crazy. So, give him the intel on the nurse I lost in Paris."

"I'll contact Nate and set it up. Send the file. We're on it."

This concludes Book 7 of Terk's Guardians: Sanders.
Read about Nate: Terk's Guardians, Book 8

Terk's Guardians: Nate (Book #8)

Nate is pulled into a mission to rescue a kidnapped woman, being held in Paris. But a normal mission versus one run by Terkel is a whole different story. Nate's first telepathic communication tells him that this will be like nothing else in his life.

During a layover in Paris, while traveling to start a job in Africa with Bullard, Madeline awoke, tied up in a strange hotel room with another female captive, named Anna. Nate comes to the rescue and shares how he had been called in to locate Madeline, when she didn't arrive as planned. Yet she wonders if she can trust him, especially when she has no recollection of who kidnapped her in the first place.

When Anna disappears again, Madeline's even more worried. What are the chances the kidnappers are looking for round two with Madeline as well?

Find Book 8 here!

To find out more visit Dale Mayer's website.

https://geni.us/DMSNate

Author's Note

Thank you for reading Sanders: Terk's Guardians, Book 7! If you enjoyed the book, please take a moment and leave a short review.

Dear reader,

I love to hear from readers, and you can contact me at my website: www.dalemayer.com or at my Facebook author page. To be informed of new releases and special offers, sign up for my newsletter or follow me on BookBub. And if you are interested in joining Dale Mayer's Reader Group, here is the Facebook sign up page.
http://geni.us/DaleMayerFBGroup

Cheers,
Dale Mayer

About the Author

Dale Mayer is a *USA Today* best-selling author, best known for her SEALs military romances, her Psychic Visions series, and her Lovely Lethal Garden cozy series. Her contemporary romances are raw and full of passion and emotion (Broken But ... Mending, Hathaway House series). Her thrillers will keep you guessing (Kate Morgan, By Death series), and her romantic comedies will keep you giggling (*It's a Dog's Life*, a stand-alone novella; and the Broken Protocols series, starring Charming Marvin, the cat).

Dale honors the stories that come to her—and some of them are crazy, break all the rules and cross multiple genres!

To go with her fiction, she also writes nonfiction in many different fields, with books available on résumé writing, companion gardening, and the US mortgage system. All her books are available in print and ebook format.

Connect with Dale Mayer Online

Dale's Website – www.dalemayer.com
Twitter – @DaleMayer
Facebook Page – geni.us/DaleMayerFBFanPage
Facebook Group – geni.us/DaleMayerFBGroup
BookBub – geni.us/DaleMayerBookbub
Instagram – geni.us/DaleMayerInstagram
Goodreads – geni.us/DaleMayerGoodreads
Newsletter – geni.us/DaleNews